**Heirs to**

*Succession, Secrets and Scandal*

Following the death of their father, English aristocrat Cedric Pemberton, it's time for the Pemberton heirs to stake their claim in the family empire.

From fashion and cosmetics to jewelry and fragrance, Aurora Inc. is a multinational company, with headquarters all over the world.

As the siblings take the lead in different divisions of the business, they'll face challenges, uncover secrets and learn to start listening to their hearts...

**Gabi and Will's Story**
*Scandal and the Runaway Bride*

**Charlotte and Jacob's Story**
*The Heiress's Pregnancy Surprise*

**Arabella and Burke's Story**
*Wedding Reunion with the Best Man*

Available now!

Dear Reader,

I'm so pleased to bring you Arabella Pemberton's story this month in the Heirs to an Empire series! Bella hasn't really stood out in the first two books. She's been in the background, being supportive, being the voice of reason, but not causing any uproar. As her cousin Christophe puts it, Bella is *la colle*—the glue that holds the family and Aurora Inc. together.

Bella has scars. Real, tangible physical ones that she's been hiding from the public for years. She knows that if she stops hiding them, it means throwing her family into the spotlight again. She also knows that finally being free of her scars means Burke Phillips will have to face his, and the last thing she wants to do is hurt Burke. She's fallen in love with him, after all.

I hope you enjoy this latest story in the series... Stay tuned, as there are more Pembertons who need their happy-ever-afters!

Best wishes,

*Donna*

# Wedding Reunion with the Best Man

—

### Donna Alward

Recycling programs
for this product may
not exist in your area.

ISBN-13: 978-1-335-56698-0

Wedding Reunion with the Best Man

Copyright © 2021 by Donna Alward

This edition published by arrangement with Harlequin Books S.A.

For questions and comments about the quality of this book, please contact us at CustomerService@Harlequin.com.

Harlequin Enterprises ULC
22 Adelaide St. West, 40th Floor
Toronto, Ontario M5H 4E3, Canada
www.Harlequin.com

Printed in U.S.A.

**Donna Alward** lives on Canada's east coast with her family, which includes her husband, a couple of kids, a senior dog and two zany cats. Her heartwarming stories of love, hope and homecoming have been translated into several languages, hit bestseller lists and won awards, but her favorite thing is hearing from readers! When she's not writing, she enjoys reading (of course), knitting, gardening, cooking...and she is a *Masterpiece* addict. You can visit her on the web at donnaalward.com and join her mailing list at donnaalward.com/newsletter.

**Praise for
Donna Alward**

"Ms. Alward wrote a beautiful love story that is not to be missed. She provided a tale rich with emotions, filled with sexual chemistry, wonderful dialogue, and endearing characters.... I highly recommend *Beauty and the Brooding Billionaire* to other readers."

—*Goodreads*

# CHAPTER ONE

ARABELLA PEMBERTON LIFTED her hair off her neck for a brief moment, fluttering it a bit to cool the skin beneath. Italy in July was nearly unbearable. Why William and Gabi had chosen to wed in the hottest month of the year escaped her. But here she was, in the Baresi villa in Umbria, preparing to be one of Gabi's bridesmaids. She was thrilled her little brother had found such happiness, and she adored Gabi. She just hated the heat, especially with her thick hair and ever-present long sleeves.

No one in the family ever questioned her hairstyles or her proclivity for garments that covered her past the elbows. They all knew it was to cover the scars she bore. As a Pemberton and a member of the Aurora Inc. dynasty, she was often photographed. The last thing she ever wanted was for the press to get wind of the dozens of cuts on her neck and arms. The worst were on her arms. The few on her face she covered with a precise makeup regimen. It was no accident that she now headed up the cosmetics division of Aurora Inc.

That one moment in time, the one night she'd been stupid and foolish, had now marked her forever. It had robbed her of so much, particularly in the friend and romance departments. Her worst fear was that she'd trust someone and they would share her closely guarded secret. In a business where image was everything, she didn't want to bring that kind of attention to Aurora, and, if she were being honest, she never wanted to relive that night and the weeks of pain and anguish that followed.

Which made this week particularly difficult.

She let her hair back down on her neck and fought the urge to scratch. For the entire week, Burke Phillips would be here, too. William's college chum and best man. Why William couldn't choose Stephen or Christophe to be best man was beyond her. Her brother and cousin were suitable choices. But oh, no. He had to ask Burke, because even though they hadn't seen each other in over a year, this was apparently a "thing."

She'd successfully managed to avoid Burke for the past twelve years. They'd both been seventeen, and Burke had been visiting Chatsworth Manor with his father, then the Viscount Downham. Even though William had been two years younger than Burke, the pair had hit it off. William had gone off to the same university as Burke and they had become fast friends. Until university ended, anyway, and Burke had gone his way and William had…well, William had had a rough few years.

Now Burke was here. And he was one of only two other people who understood what had happened the night she'd gotten those scars.

"Bella, are you coming down?" That was Gabi's voice, and Bella knew she was running late for lunch.

"I'll be right there," she called back. She turned from the window and checked her reflection in the mirror. It was so hot she'd actually wondered if her makeup had melted, but no, everything was still in place. While there was no air-conditioning at the villa, she couldn't deny that the room was lovely. Her window looked out over an olive grove, and the bed and furniture were absolutely beautiful. It was Gabi's sister's room, but Giulia had offered to stay with her boyfriend, Marco, to make room for some of William's family.

The Baresis were wonderful, generous, fun people.

She made her way down the steps to the bottom floor, where a table was set up buffet-style for lunch. Signora Baresi was a fabulous cook and knew how to put on a marvelous spread. Thankfully, it was also a little cooler downstairs. Bella grabbed a plate and began to fill it with an array of vegetables and meats. With a full house leading up to the wedding, the casual approach to breakfast and lunch made things ever so much easier.

She'd just grabbed herself a glass of iced water when William came through the front door to the villa, calling out to everyone. "Guess who's here?" he said, coming into the kitchen with a massive smile. "Burke! Finally. The last member of the wedding party has arrived."

Bella held her breath as Burke came in behind William, his entrance a bit more subdued than Will's ebullient introduction. "Everyone, this is Burke Phillips. Burke, these are Gabi's parents, Massimo and Lucia Baresi, and Gabi's sister, Giulia, and her boyfriend, Marco. And of course you've met my family before. Stephen and Maman are in Perugia today, but you know Christophe, and my sisters Charlotte and Bella."

Bella was last, and Burke's gaze lingered on her. Even that much was too much. It didn't matter that it had been over a decade. He knew. He knew what had happened and he knew the horror of it, and it showed in his eyes as they looked at each other.

"Bella," he said softly.

"Hello, Burke."

Will was oblivious to everything but his happiness, so he pulled Burke ahead and Burke shook hands with everyone and then he was given a plate. Food was truly a language of love here, she realized, standing to the side while conversation and laughter filled the room. Massimo, now through his cancer treatments and remarkably robust, was already expounding on the greatness of Umbrian meats to Burke, who had a shocking amount of food on his plate. It was their way of making him welcome, she realized. The Baresis were wonderful. No wonder Stephen and William had warmed to them so much.

She found a slightly quieter corner in which to sit, and picked at the food on her plate. It was a surprise, then, when a shadow appeared at her shoulder and Burke's voice touched her ears.

"May I join you, Bella?"

It was the only free seat in the room; how could she deny him? "Please do," she invited, not unkindly, but not enthusiastically, either.

An awkward silence fell over them, making Bella shift in her seat. "Your trip was satisfactory?" she asked, then chided herself for sounding so stilted.

"It was fine. A hop, skip and a jump to Italy, anyway. You?"

"Most of us arrived two days ago. I'm sure the Baresis will be glad when the commotion is over."

He looked over at the table, where Signora Baresi was laughing. "Maybe. But they seem to be enjoying it so far."

"They wouldn't hear of us staying at a hotel."

"I know. I'm at Marco's with William. No keeping the bride and groom together, I guess."

At least they wouldn't be under the same roof.

He picked at his food and then looked up at her, his dark eyes assessing. "You look good, Bella."

Heat crept up her already too-warm neck. "Thank you. I hear you're working in London at the moment."

"Yes, at St. Thomas's."

It had surprised her to hear that Burke had gone on to become a doctor and then pursued a cardiac specialty. It was a rather serious profession for a boy who'd been keen on partying and who had every advantage, including money and title. For he wasn't just Burke Phillips anymore, he was also Viscount Downham.

"You like it there?"

"I do. Very much."

"And do they address you as milord?" She was only half teasing, and his smile faded as his gaze held hers.

"No," he replied. "Bella, I know that—"

"I shouldn't have asked that," she interrupted. "It was rude of me. Sorry." No longer hungry, she rose and took her plate with her. "I just remembered I have a fitting this afternoon. Enjoy your lunch."

She walked away, her tummy quivering not only because it was Burke but because she'd just

told a bald-faced lie about being busy. She didn't
want him to be nice to her. Didn't want him to
be here at all. For the rest of the week, she'd have
to try to avoid him. But she could do it, because
she was used to making adjustments to avoid un-
pleasant situations. She doubted her family even
noticed anymore, she'd become so adept at it.
Of all the Pembertons, she was the one most in
the background, and that was just how she liked
it. Let Stephen and Charlotte be the faces in the
magazines and online. She was content behind
the scenes, working for the company she loved.
Holding things together.

It was one week. She'd built the life she
wanted—well, mostly wanted—and she wouldn't
let Burke mess that up for her. No matter how
handsome or charming he was.

For the rest of the afternoon, Bella stayed in her
unbearably hot room, laptop open, answering
work emails and sending instructions to her assistant. The new cosmetics line, Naturel, had
launched earlier in the year and was doing very
well. It was the first line for Aurora that was
completely vegan and responsibly sourced, and
Bella was hugely proud of that. It was also the
first real innovation she'd been in charge of at the
company, and so she wanted to keep tabs on everything that was happening in the division. She
tried very hard to pull her weight. All of them

did, really. It still surprised her that Maman had given each child a position of great responsibility, but she always said that her children would rise to the task. It was great to have that faith, but it was also scary as heck. None of them wanted to fail and disappoint the great Aurora Germain-Pemberton.

Dinner was another lively, large affair. Huge dishes of vegetable-stuffed cannelloni filled the table, along with the ever-present bread. Everyone filled their plates and then went outside to the patio, where several tables had been put together to form one very long banquet-style table. Wine bottles punctuated the tabletop, both red and white so people could choose depending on preference. Bella found herself next to Charlotte, who passed on the wine. "Do you miss it?" Bella asked with a smile as she poured a vibrant red into her glass.

Charlotte touched her tummy, which had a small but noticeable bump. "Not really. It's worth it."

Charlotte was absolutely radiant in her pregnancy. "When does Jacob arrive?" Charlotte and Jacob were still glowing from their garden wedding only a month earlier.

"Thursday. He's working until then."

Conversation halted as Massimo made a toast, and then everyone dug in. As Bella ate, she pondered Charlotte and Jacob's relationship. It had been a whirlwind that resulted in a surprise pregnancy, but her sister was blissfully happy. So was William, with Gabi. And Bella was more than happy for them, but seeing her siblings step into marital bliss made her painfully aware that she probably never would.

And that was on her. To be in an intimate relationship meant letting someone see all the ugliness. No thanks.

The somber thought guided her gaze down the table to where Burke sat, close to William. She could tell the two were recounting some of their exploits as students, and those seated around them were laughing. She took the time to study him. He'd grown from a slightly lanky, good-looking boy to a devastatingly handsome man. His dark hair held a hint of curl that gave him a boyish look, and his golden-brown eyes were more serious than she remembered. Or if not more serious… She paused. Today, when she'd looked at him, she'd sensed depths that made her wonder what joys and sorrows he'd experienced, because his eyes were…soulful, she realized. It was what made him hard to resist.

Perhaps he still had his own scars from that night.

"Bella? Aren't you going to eat?"

Charlotte's voice drew her back to the present. She hadn't even touched her food, so she dutifully cut into the cannelloni and took a scrumptious bite. "Sorry," she said, after she'd chewed and swallowed. "I got distracted."

"By Burke? He's very handsome."

"No, not by Burke," she replied, a little sharply. "It's just a lot of people. That's all."

Charlotte's brows pulled together and Bella knew why. They were almost always around a lot of people and it had never bothered Bella before, as long as she was covered. Now she'd lied to her sister and Charlotte had seen right through it.

When dinner was over, Bella insisted on helping clean up. She needed something to keep her busy and out of Burke's sphere.

It was going to be a long week, wasn't it?

Burke watched as Bella escaped into the house with Signora Baresi and Giulia on the premise of helping clean up after the meal. There'd been nearly a dozen of them for dinner, and the mess was no trifling matter. He rose from his seat and started collecting empty wine bottles.

"You don't need to help," William said, looking up at him with a smile.

Burke raised an eyebrow. "Well, Mr. Lord of the Manor, there's no staff here, is there? And I'm too enlightened to think this is something that is left to the women."

"Going to get dishpan hands, are we?"

Burke hesitated. "Probably not. I don't think

your sister wants me anywhere near the kitchen right now."

William's eyes lost their teasing and he looked Burke in the eye. "I had hoped it wouldn't be this way. She's avoided you for ten years."

"Twelve, really, but who's counting?"

He gave up picking up bottles and sat beside William. He, too, had hoped that things wouldn't be awkward between him and Bella. "Will, I don't know what to say to her. We've never talked about the accident."

"I don't know, Burke," William said thoughtfully. "Part of me thinks you should come right out and deal with it together. Another part says let it alone."

"Same," Burke replied with a sigh. He waited a moment and then said what had been on his mind since arriving in Italy. "Did you ask me to be your best man so that I would have to talk to her?"

William shook his head. "Actually, I almost *didn't* ask you for that very reason. But it's my wedding. My only wedding, and I wanted you to be part of it. You've been my friend through so much."

"Not always. Not when you were in rehab."

"Not your fault I didn't tell you what a mess I was in. And you were in med school at the time. You would have been there if I'd asked. I was too ashamed, and so that's on me."

Burke looked at his friend and admired all he'd overcome to be the whole, happy human being he was now. Certainly more whole than Burke was at the moment. He couldn't fault Arabella for hanging on to the memories of the accident when he hadn't been able to escape them, either.

A boy had died. Arabella had been in hospital for weeks. And Burke and the other girl, Fiona, had sustained their own minor injuries.

He should have stopped Royce from driving that night. Should have kept Bella from getting in the car. Hell, he and Fiona shouldn't have tagged along. But they had all been young and bullet-proof.

"She's never forgiven me for the accident," Burke said quietly.

William didn't answer. He looked as if he wanted to say something but was holding back. "What is it?" Burke asked.

"Nothing. Honestly, this is between you and Bella. If you two decide to talk it out this week, great. If not, I'm still thrilled you're here as my best man. Maybe you could try to not be so serious for once, as well. Take off your doctor face and have a good time. We're in Italy, man. Great food, wonderful company…a wedding. Lighten up a bit."

Irritation flared but Burke tamped it down. It wasn't that William was wrong, it was that turning off that driven part of him wasn't like flicking off a light switch. He needed time to wind down. It was hard to do that when Bella was right in front of him, a reminder of why he'd gone into medicine in the first place.

"I'll try," was all he said, and he got up again to finish collecting the bottles. "I'll take these inside."

When he entered the kitchen, he walked into a bunch of happy chatter that made him pause as a warm feeling settled over him. It reminded him of his two sisters and his mother, taking over the kitchen from the staff to bake Christmas cookies or a special birthday cake. The sound of their laughter had made him feel secure at a time when everything was chaos in his brain. First, the accident. And then, while he was in college, the aneurysm that had taken his father suddenly and brutally, shoving Burke into the role of viscount. And Lord, all the secrets in between. It was the secrets that ate at him the most.

He'd become responsible for the family at a time he was barely responsible for himself, and carried the secrets with him. Not a single person in the world knew that he'd discovered his father's affair, taking the man from hero in Burke's eyes to a cheat and a liar. It had been a heavy, heavy burden. Still was, even now.

But that happy laughter, the warm sound of female voices chatting over a menial task…it was healing in a "life goes on and everything's okay" way. It was how his mother had gotten them through those early days of grief, and something about it wrapped around his heart and squeezed.

"Burke?" Gabi appeared before him.

"Hmm?"

"Thanks for bringing the wine bottles in. Hey, Bella, can you show Burke to the pantry? We can put the empty bottles in there until later."

"Oh, uh, sure," Bella replied, and wiped her hands on a dish towel. She didn't meet his eyes, but instead led the way to a small room off the kitchen that held a shop's worth of merchandise, it seemed.

He followed her inside, and she pointed to an empty shelf. "I guess you can put them there."

He moved to put them on the shelf and bobbled one; she rushed forward and took it from his hands before placing it carefully beside the others. "Thanks," he murmured.

"You're welcome."

The close atmosphere of the pantry lent an intimacy to the moment that was unexpected. When Bella turned to leave, he reached out and caught her wrist lightly. "Bella, wait. Please."

She stilled. Not in a comfortable way, but like an animal that was trapped. Why? Was she so angry at him that the very idea of being in a room with him repulsed her?

"I should get back."

"Just give me one minute. Please, Bella. We haven't spoken since—"

"I know since when," she interrupted sharply. "We don't need to discuss it."

"Yes," he said firmly, "we do. Because ever since then you've avoided me and even now you can't meet my eyes."

She looked up at him, dark eyes sharp and defiant. So she could look at him. But with annoyance that built a shield. Nothing vulnerable. Guilt threaded through him again at the knowledge that he could have prevented what had happened if he'd been more responsible.

"I'm sorry," he said simply. "That is what I wanted to say. I'm sorry I failed everyone that night. I should never have allowed Royce to get behind the wheel. I shouldn't have gotten in that car and I should have kept you from getting into it, too."

She looked away. So much for meeting his eyes.

"Thank you for your apology," she muttered, pulling her wrist away from his fingers.

That was all he was going to get. A thank-you but no absolving him of the part he'd played. Not just the accident but the events of the evening leading up to it. Finally giving her the apology she deserved did nothing to alleviate his guilt or remorse. If anything, he felt worse.

She went to the door of the pantry, putting

extra space between them. "Thank you for apologizing. But some things you just can't undo, Burke."

She left him standing there, more conflicted than ever.

# CHAPTER TWO

THE FOLLOWING DAY Bella went with Gabi, Charlotte, and Giulia into Perugia to shop. It was a relief to get away from the villa for a while—and any thought of Burke. Today's excursion schedule was a final fitting for their dresses, a boutique where they planned to splurge on lingerie, lunch, and picking up the tiny organza bags that contained wedding favors—sugared almonds—for each guest.

Bella loved her dress. All three bridesmaids had similar dresses, the same pale blue chiffon, but each had chosen a favored neckline and sleeve and one of the Aurora designers had done the rest. Charlotte, with her gorgeous collarbones, slim shoulders and slightly popping belly, had picked an Empire waist style with cute cap sleeves that fluttered. Giulia, the youngest of them all and with a slightly athletic shape, went for a halter-style that tied at the nape of her neck and sent ribbons of chiffon cascading down her back. Bella had gone with a soft vee that plunged to her cleavage, and long sleeves that came to narrow cuffs at her wrist but stayed cool due to the filmy fabric. Each dress fell to the floor in delicate folds, and they'd all be wearing shoes that Charlotte had designed and had made for the occasion. Bella wouldn't be surprised if Charlotte spearheaded a footwear line at Aurora one of these days, leaving her PR title behind.

Charlotte knew Bella's reason for the long sleeves, and there were times Bella wondered if Will had told Gabi and Giulia because neither woman had asked, even though sleeves during summer was a bit odd. She didn't want to inquire, though, because if he hadn't said anything, she would then have to explain.

Once they were all dressed, they stepped out together and Gabi put her hand to her mouth.

"Oh, you all look beautiful!" She glanced at the seamstress. "What do you think? Is that a little pucker in Charlotte's bodice?"

Charlotte sighed. "Ugh. My figure changes every day, I think! If it's not my belly, it's my breasts."

Bella laughed. "And you love every minute of it."

"I do," Charlotte admitted. "Especially now that the queasiness has gone."

The seamstress had her let out a breath and then made an adjustment. "That should do it," she remarked, stepping back and nodding with approval. "You—" she pointed at Giulia "—are at that glorious age that makes a sack look wonderful. Yours is perfect." She turned her attention to Bella, and Bella's stomach twisted. She hoped there wouldn't be anything intrusive. She should have taken the dress home and let Maman do the pinning. Bella was adept enough she could do the alterations herself.

"The waist is still slightly too big."

Bella looked at the woman and said confidently, "No more than a quarter of an inch."

"*Si, si*. You are right." Thankfully the woman didn't come closer with her pins and get up close and personal.

"I don't want to take it off," Giulia admitted. "It's so beautiful."

"And you'll be able to wear it in a few days," Gabi said. "The flowers are going to look gorgeous with it."

Bella couldn't help but get swept away in the excited energy. Giulia did a swirl with her skirt, revealing the creamy white heels, and said, "And I get to be on Burke's arm. He is *molto bello*." She wiggled her eyebrows a little and laughed.

Bella's Italian wasn't great, but she came back with a dry, *"Bello è altrettanto bello."*

*Handsome is as handsome does.*

The women burst out laughing. Charlotte nudged Bella's arm. "Come on, Bel. You have to admit he's pretty gorgeous. And I think he likes you. Otherwise what were you doing in the pantry last night?"

Bella, having grown up with two brothers, a sister and a cousin, was no stranger to sibling teasing. Though her stomach twisted anxiously, she answered with a "wouldn't you like to know?" And then, at the increased laughter, she added, "Don't worry. Nothing happened that kept me up at night."

Nothing except that apology. He'd been so sincere, and she'd wanted to say it was okay. She didn't blame him for what happened. And yet she lived with the scars every day, and truthfully, she just didn't want to have to deal with him at all.

After the fittings they went to the lingerie boutique. While they each shopped for themselves, the three bridesmaids had agreed that they wanted to buy Gabi a nightgown for her wedding night. After several gowns had gone into the change room, Gabi finally found the one she wanted. "It's…well…" she said from behind the curtain, her voice a little hesitant.

"Come out," Giulia said. "We want to see it."

Again with a slightly nervous laugh. But Gabi pushed aside the curtain and the three women stood speechless for five full seconds.

*"Dio mio!"* This from Giulia. "Gabriella. That is going to knock his eyeballs out."

Bella looked at the gown with envy. It was a flowy column of sheer lace, with a narrow halter tie at the neck and a back that dipped right to Gabi's tailbone. There were no panels of solid material to cover anything, though a tiny bit of the lace pattern appeared to hide Gabi's nipples and she wore simple thong underwear. It was the sexiest thing Bella had ever seen.

She tried to imagine wearing such a thing and knew she never would. Not with the marks criss-crossing her arms. Or the one on the back of her neck. She didn't begrudge Gabi a moment of this. But she could be happy for her friend and soon-to-be sister-in-law and still harbor a little resentment toward life's circumstances.

"It's amazing, Gabi," she said. "I mean, I don't necessarily like thinking of my brother in times like this, but Giulia's right. His tongue is going to hit the floor."

Gabi blushed. "If there's any night I'd really like to surprise him, this is it."

"Then it's yours, from us," Charlotte decreed. "Our wedding gift to you."

They took their bags and stored everything in the trunk of Gabi's car, then headed to lunch at a small restaurant in Perugia's historic district where they dined on mixed salad, gnocchi with saffron and truffles, and a *semifreddo* with Perugia's signature Baci chocolates. As they finished with strong coffee, Bella found herself hoping tonight's dinner was on the lighter side. Especially if her dress was to be taken in for the wedding.

One last errand for the sugared almond wedding favors and they were on their way back to the Baresi villa.

When they arrived, the family was outside on the patio, and Stephen, William, Burke, and Marco were in the pool, cooling off. There was little swimming going on; instead, the men each had a floating chair and they were holding drinks in their hands, the picture of total relaxation.

"You're back! Come in. Water's perfect."

Charlotte shut down the challenge. "The last time I was in a pool with you two, you dunked me under water. No thanks."

"And I just had my hair colored yesterday. No pool water for me," said Gabi.

Giulia stepped up. "I will. Just let me change."

"How about you, Bella?" That was from Burke.

The patio seemed to go quiet, and Bella knew why, but she smiled and politely declined. "No thanks. Though I might dip my toes in."

"Spoilsport."

She laughed. "I've been called worse."

They took their packages inside, then returned to the patio for cool drinks in the shade. A light breeze blew over the hilltop, cooling the sheen of sweat on Bella's chest and arms. How she wished she really didn't care about her scars and could just slip on a bathing suit like Giulia and jump into the water without a care in the world. If it were just her siblings, she would. But not in front of people who weren't family. Who hadn't already seen.

When the heat was nearly unbearable, she went poolside and did indeed slip her feet into the water. The water came halfway up her calves, and she decided that later tonight she'd sneak out and go for a swim after dark. Nothing was so noticeable then, and everyone would be in bed. Maybe it would help her sleep better. Last night she'd had a fan to at least create some air movement, but she'd still slept without any covers and just her light nightgown.

Burke swam over and looked up at her, water sparkling on his lashes. "You sure you won't come in?"

"This is perfect," she replied. "And no having to mess with my hair afterward."

"I know, I have that problem, too," he quipped, running his hand over his short curls. She couldn't help it, she laughed.

Then he swam away, dipping under the water like a playful seal and emerging twenty feet away, directly beneath William's floating chair, sending William tumbling into the water.

Everyone burst out laughing at William's yell and subsequent spluttering as he surfaced, rubbing his hand over his face.

Burke looked over at her and winked, and despite the cool water on her legs, she went warm all over.

*No*, she told herself. *Not again.*

Twelve years ago, she'd been so taken with him. The ripe age of seventeen, a summer party, a handsome boy, both of them enjoying their last weeks before university. He'd been an incorrigible flirt but hadn't paid a whit of attention to her. He'd found a chum in William, and all the girls at the party had been curious and fawning over him. It had stung more than a little that he'd flirted with everyone *but* her.

Bella had tried twice to engage him in conversation, but he'd listened with half an ear, nodding politely and not really paying attention. She'd tossed her hair over her shoulder and sent him come-hither looks. Nothing.

So for him to wink at her now hurt, when she would have given anything for a smattering of attention from him as a teenager.

There was a huge splash as Marco picked up Giulia and threw her in the pool, and Bella got up before she ended up getting a good soaking. And just as she had yesterday, she escaped inside with the excuse of keeping tabs on work, while she felt the gazes of everyone on her back.

She went back to the pool when she was fairly sure everyone was in bed. William's car was still here, and she imagined he was stealing moments with Gabi, since they were staying in different houses until the big day. But the house was silent, and she tiptoed out dressed in her bathing suit with a light robe over top and carrying a towel. An elastic band was around her wrist; once she was at the pool she'd anchor her mass of hair into a messy bun to keep it from being cumbersome.

The lights outside were off, which suited her just fine. There was enough moonlight to guide her way, and she shrugged out of her robe, leaving it draped across a chair. She put the towel on the seat and slipped out of her sandals. Then she stepped quietly into the water, holding on to the stair railing and easing herself into the cool relief it provided.

Oh, heavenly. The cloying heat that was in the top floor of the Baresi villa disappeared from her skin as the cool water instantly soothed. She anchored her hair as best she could, though small tendrils still trailed along her neck and framed her face. With a sigh, Bella sank up to her shoulders, closing her eyes and loving the soft way the water moved over her skin.

She struck out in a gentle crawl, headed to the other end of the pool, then turned and swam back again. She changed to a breaststroke and kept swimming lengths until she was breathing hard and had had enough exertion. Then she lay on her back and floated, staring up at the stars.

"I didn't think you were the kind to indulge in midnight swims," came a voice, and she broke her float and stood in the pool, startled to be caught when she had been sure there was no one around. The water came to her chest; she quickly bent her legs so it covered her to her neck and made it look as if she were treading water.

Burke. "What are you doing here? I mean, aren't you supposed to be at Marco's?"

He went to the edge of the pool and sat, casually pulled his sandals off, and put his feet in the water just as she had earlier. "Marco left with Giulia, Christophe, and Stephen. Your mother has gone to bed, and William asked if I'd hang around so we could drive back together later. I said sure and took the opportunity to go for a late stroll in the olive groves."

She frowned. "Why would he ask you to stay?" Once it was out of her mouth, she knew it sounded rude and heat crept up her cool cheeks.

Burke merely raised an eyebrow. "Accountability, apparently. Might be a little too easy to 'fall asleep' and end up staying over. If he still has to take me back to Marco's…"

She couldn't help it, she snickered a little. "I can't believe what a stickler William is being for this kind of thing."

"I know. In uni he was always up for some trouble. Now he's on the straight and narrow." Burke leaned back on his hands and moved his feet in the water, creating little waves that purled over his feet. "But he'll do anything for Gabi, and this is what she wants, so here I am, putting in time, just like I used to when he'd end up with some girl at a pub and I'd be left—"

"With your own girl," she finished for him, a smile curving her lips. "Will's told me the stories, too, you know. If you're going to play all innocent, at least pick someone who might believe you."

She was teasing him and probably shouldn't be. After all, she was stuck in the pool until he moved on. Even in the moonlight, the ugly crisscross of scars would be visible. She didn't want him to see them. Ever.

He was laughing now, the sound warm and smooth, like the amaretto she'd sipped after dinner tonight. The sound faded away in the soft breeze, and her stomach started getting all swirly…both with nerves that he wasn't going to leave, and with anticipation of him staying.

And yet long ago, he'd been the one to turn away and barely look at her. Maybe he didn't deserve her attention now.

And maybe, just maybe, she should stop having hurt feelings about that night. They'd been kids and he hadn't been into her. So what? What happened after he'd shunned her had been a hundred percent her decision, after all.

"Aren't you getting cold?"

She shook her head quickly. "Actually, no. My room is on the top floor and very hot. I came out to cool off and hopefully sleep a little better."

He nodded. "William said Gabi's been after her father to install air-conditioning for years."

"It's no big deal. I just thought a swim would be perfect."

"Hmm." He tapped his lips. "Maybe I should join you."

Her good humor turned to ice as her body froze. "You don't have your swimsuit on."

He pulled his feet out of the water and started to stand. "Who needs a swimsuit?"

Bella's lips dropped open in dismay. "You are not coming in here…without clothes."

"Bella. Would I do such a thing?"

That was the problem. She didn't really know, and her own mind and body betrayed her because she desperately wanted to find out. Burke pulled his T-shirt off and dropped it on the same chair as her towel and robe. He reached into his pocket and pulled out his wallet and phone, putting them on top of his T-shirt. And then he jumped in the water with a giant splash.

He was in the pool with her. In his shorts, thank God. But still. The wave from his plunge went over her shoulder and into her surprised mouth, and she coughed and spluttered. "I can't believe you did that!" she exclaimed when he surfaced about ten feet away. She coughed again.

His grin was boyish and his close-cropped curls were flat and dark against his head. "I haven't done anything impulsive in a long time.

If this is the extent of my surprising behavior, I think I'm still okay."

"You're crazy."

"Probably."

She had to get out of the pool. She was actually enjoying this, but it was too risky. The last thing she needed was for Burke to get too close. To see her skin. To ask questions.

"I—I need to go," she said, backing up a few steps. But she backed up in the wrong direction and stepped onto the slope of where the deep end started. Her foot slipped and she lost her balance, sliding under the water briefly before popping back up. To her dismay, Burke was less than three feet away, reaching for her with his hand.

"I'm fine. Just slipped on the bottom."

He took another step and circled her wrist with his fingers. "That's okay. I've got you." He gave her arm a slight tug and pulled her closer. His dark eyes found hers, and a snap of attraction flashed between them. No. This wasn't okay. She shouldn't want him so much.

"Let me go, Burke."

He did. As soon as she made the request, he dropped her arm and her feet touched the bottom again. Bella knew she should move away, so why wasn't she? She was standing now, with her shoulders above the water, and his gaze dropped to her skin and his lips opened in shock.

"Arabella."

The way he said her name hit her like a brick. "No," she said firmly, starting to walk away, the resistance of the water against her legs making it slower going than she wanted. "I need to go in."

This time he followed her and when he reached for her arm, he didn't let go. "Bella. That…that's what happened to you?"

"Don't," she said. "I already hear the pity in your voice and I don't want it."

"Too bad," he said firmly. "And I'm not pitying you, not really. It doesn't mean I can't be sorry that this happened."

She met his gaze. "When we crashed, I was foolish. I could feel us start to flip and I covered my head with my arms, like I would on a plane, you know? So when the windows shattered, all the glass went into my arms and the back of my neck. Thank God the airbag didn't deploy. I would have taken the brunt of that force right on my head."

He wasn't touching her now. The ladder was only a half dozen steps away, but she stayed where she was. Maybe it was time to not run and just say it. "The glass left me with scars that will never go away. The few on my face are smaller and I had plastic surgery, and I cover them as best I can."

"I never noticed."

"That's very deliberate."

Quiet fell between them for a few moments,

and then finally he asked, his voice soft with concern, "Do they still hurt?"

She shook her head, feeling a familiar stinging behind her eyes and willing it away. "No. Actually, the scar tissue makes it so I don't have as much sensitivity there as I might otherwise. It's kind of…numb."

"And that's why you always wear the long sleeves. And your hair down."

He'd noticed. She nodded.

He turned away briefly, the water swishing along his rib cage. Bella gave him time. After all, he'd been in the car, too. He must have some memories of that night.

"I didn't see you when the ambulance came."

"You were unconscious. It…" She swallowed. "It scared me something awful. I was afraid you were dead like…like Royce." She hated when that image flashed into her head. Royce had been the one to finally take an interest in her and she'd returned the interest just to show Burke what he was missing.

"The girl I was with, Fiona. She just had minor injuries."

"Yeah. But you and I…we were on the side that took the impact of the roll." Her heart rate was climbing as it always did if she let herself go back to that night. "And Royce…he didn't wear his seat belt."

She could see the crash site as if it were yesterday. The crumpled car. Fiona screaming in panic. Royce's body and Burke unresponsive. Her own blood. Bella started to shake. "I can't do this," she said quickly, rushing to the steps. She climbed out and ran to the chair with the towel, but Burke was close behind her.

"Bella, stop. Wait."

She grabbed the towel and tried to dry herself quickly so she could cover herself with her robe again. Her loose bun was now drooping nearly to her neck, lopsided, and she wished the blasted moon would go beneath a cloud rather than glowing down on them like a spotlight.

He retrieved her robe and gently put it over her shoulders, as if he understood her panic. The gentleness of it nearly tore her apart. Her family knew. They'd gone through the pain of recovery with her. But she had no desire to let anyone else in. It was too…ugly.

And then he did something utterly unexpected. He folded her into his arms.

His skin was cold from the water, and yet there was a heat to his body that she couldn't deny, even as the water from his skin dampened spots on her robe. She held her body stiffly, unsure of what to do with the compassionate contact, for it truly was kind and not sexual. Maybe sexual would have been easier to fight against.

"I'm sorry," he murmured close to her ear. "I'm so sorry."

"I said I don't want your pity." She attempted to pull away, but he tightened his arms.

"That's not what I mean. That night…"

And then he let out a shuddering sigh and she realized that she needed to consider he had been hurt as well. So she tentatively put her arms around his waist and let him hug her.

When he finally let her go, she looked up at him and squared her shoulders. "I don't want to talk about this again," she said firmly. "It's over and it's done. I'm fine, you see. So let's just get through this wedding and then you'll go back to your life at the hospital and I'll go back to mine in Paris and that will be that."

His eyes clouded with confusion. "Bella, I—"

"No, Burke. Please."

And then she turned and finally ran away, back into the house and upstairs to her room, where she took off her robe, stared at the white slashes of scar tissue, and cried.

# CHAPTER THREE

BURKE WAS SITTING on the chair, his head in his hands, when William finally came out of the house at nearly 1:00 a.m.

"Sorry I took so long. I'm a horrible friend."

Burke looked up and tried a smile. "It's fine. It's your wedding in a few days. You're entitled."

William's smile faded. "What's wrong?"

Burke wasn't sure what to say. He put off answering by getting up and tucking the chair back under the table. William started laughing. "Your shorts are wet. Did you fall in the pool?"

"I jumped in. After your sister."

William's laugh came to an abrupt halt. "With Bella? And you survived?"

Burke finally met William's gaze, and he found himself more than a bit angry. "You should have told me, Will."

They started walking toward Will's car. "You saw, then." Will's voice was guarded.

"She didn't want me to. I had no idea. That she…" He couldn't speak for a moment.

He'd tried not to show his shock, but the scars were so angry. They slashed across her skin at random angles, from her elbows to her shoulders. When she'd turned away, he'd seen one particularly bright gash on her neck. She'd been lucky it hadn't gone deeper. Even so, even in the dark he could tell it had been big enough that it had required several stitches.

He stopped and stared at Will. "We're supposed to be best friends. I was in that accident, too, Will. For God's sake, maybe I could have helped her or something!"

Will turned on him, his eyes bright. "She's my sister and she asked that we not tell a soul. I couldn't betray that request, Burke, not even for you. Not when she'd been through so much."

His stomach churned. "How much?"

"A concussion, all the stitches, several plastic surgeries. When you were released you went home with your family. Any time I saw you after that, it was in London, never at Chatsworth."

"I was too much of a coward to go back. Not for a long time, and when I finally did, Bella was never there."

"She made sure she wasn't."

That knowledge hit Burke square in the chest. She'd been avoiding him all this time. Nothing had been coincidental. No wonder her reception had been so cool, and she'd had such trouble with his apology in the pantry. His guilt doubled.

"When you asked after Bella, I said what we always said—that she was fine. Because she was. She is."

But Burke wasn't sure he agreed. Was someone who wore long sleeves even in the hottest days, who never put their hair up because of scars, actually fine? Or just pretending?

"Bella is a grown woman who can handle things her own way," William added. "It's her body."

In that Burke was in complete agreement. "You're right," he relented, releasing the tension in his shoulders. "I just…it was a shock, Will. I barely recall the accident but I remember waking up in the hospital and being so scared, hearing that Royce had died and afraid the girls had, too. None of us should have been in the car that night."

"That's true," William said. "But you weren't driving. You didn't cause the crash."

"I got in the car," Burke argued, "instead of stopping Royce when I knew he'd been drinking." Even if at the time he'd thought he'd done it for what he thought were the right reasons, it had been a huge mistake.

They'd arrived at William's car and Will stopped and put his hand on Burke's shoulder. "Look, if any of us blamed you, we wouldn't be such close friends. It was a stupid thing that happened when kids were being stupid. People have suffered enough. And you know that because I've told you that before."

"It doesn't stop the guilt, though."

"I know that feeling."

Burke knew it to be true. Their friendship had truly faltered for a few years when Will went off the rails, drinking and doing drugs. Nothing Burke could say would make Will change. In the end, it was William's brother who got him into rehab. One of the first people William had apologized to when he got out was Burke, and their friendship had healed.

"I'm sorry, Will. I'm sorry for what happened then and I'm sorry that Bella has had to endure this ever since."

"Don't feel sorry for Bella. She's a stubborn woman, smart, successful. She doesn't let what happened slow her down or keep her from getting what she wants."

As they got into the car, Burke wondered if that were true. Sure, Bella had made her decisions, but today she'd avoided the pool because of her scars, suffering in the heat instead. She'd only gone to the pool after dark when she'd be alone. He got the feeling that Bella held herself back more than people thought.

Once back at the villa owned by Marco's family, Burke escaped to his room and shed the damp shorts, hanging them over a chair to dry. He got into bed and stared at the ceiling, thinking about

Bella and wishing they'd talked long ago. He was
sure she still held on to the trauma of that night;
her blatant refusal to talk about it said that loud
and clear. Had she gone through therapy? People handled things in different ways. He had his
mum to thank for booking him sessions with a
therapist when he'd started having nightmares
in the months following the accident. And going
into medicine wasn't a random thing. He'd felt
such a burning need to help people after he'd experienced competent, loving care from his doctors and nurses.

How had Bella handled it all? Beyond covering her scars as if they didn't exist?

The thought kept him up long into the night.

For the next two days, Burke noticed that Bella
did whatever she could to avoid being near him.
She either sought protection in a group, which
wasn't difficult considering the number of people around, or disappeared with the excuse of
keeping up with work. Oddly enough, the other
Pemberton family members didn't seem half as
concerned with work as she did.

On Thursday, Charlotte's husband, Jacob, arrived from London. Burke took one look at him,
looked at Will, and said, "That guy looks like a
Viking."

"He can kick your ass," Christophe said, moving to stand by Burke's other side.

Burke snorted, still watching as the big blond captured Charlotte in a hug. "He's the bodyguard, right?"

"Former SAS. We hired his firm to watch over Charlotte during Fashion Week last February."

Burke couldn't contain his grin. "He did that and then some, it looks like. Charlotte's beaming. Good for them."

"Come on, I'll introduce you. He's really a very nice guy."

Introductions were made, including a very firm handshake, and then Stephen said, "I guess we can have our stag night now that Jacob's finally here."

William turned his head in confusion. "Stag night? I didn't think we were doing that."

Burke grinned and clapped William on the shoulder. "Of course we are. It's my sacred duty as best man, after all. I have it all planned. Jacob, I hope you haven't put your passport away."

At William's stunned look, Burke burst out laughing. "Don't worry. We're not going to do anything that'll get you in trouble with your bride." There'd be none of that foolishness with women and last chances to sow wild oats. Those careless, selfish acts could ruin relationships.

Giulia bounced over. "And we're having what Bella has called a hen night, anyway. Marco helped us set it up at a vineyard near Siena. One of his friends."

Burke's gaze flew to where Bella was standing, wearing a pair of skinny white jeans and a flowy top that draped over her arms. She hadn't spoken to him since dashing off from the pool in the moonlight. Today she'd pulled her hair back from her face but the rest of her dark waves fell down her back, like an inky waterfall. She was so beautiful. Perhaps even more beautiful to him now that he understood all she'd endured.

As if she felt his eyes on her, she turned and their gazes met. That electrifying jolt of recognition was still between them. How inconvenient. As she looked away and spoke to Signora Baresi, he realized that being attracted to her wasn't what he wanted at all. What he wanted was absolution. But how could he ask for it when she had to live with her scars every day? It was hardly fair.

A hand clapped him on the back and he turned to find Will smiling at him. "A stag? You and your surprises."

Burke shook away the thoughts of Bella and smiled at his happy friend. "Tuxedos required," he replied. "We're headed to Monte Carlo. You'd better go pack and include a lucky charm."

Bella looked around her at the gorgeous vineyard and let out a sigh as the tension drained from her body. For the next eighteen hours, the female portion of the bridal party was going to be enjoying a wine and spa trip to get ready for the wedding. She had her own room—with air-conditioning—that overlooked the stunning Tuscan hills. Soon the Pemberton and Baresi ladies would be pampered with their choice of treatments: facials, manicures, pedicures, massages, wraps…whatever their hearts desired. There was a hot tub and a sauna as well, and a gorgeous dinner planned.

Bella knew that a typical hen night might include pub hopping and a more…unrestrained atmosphere. But when she and Charlotte had asked Giulia what Gabi would want, Giulia had known exactly what to do.

That's what sisters did, really. They knew each other. So she sought out her own.

Bella found Charlotte sitting outside on a patio, the light breeze ruffling her hair as she sipped a glass of sparking water. "I think Giulia and Gabi are still getting settled," Charlotte said. "You know it's cruel for Jacob to arrive only for us to be dragged apart again."

Bella smiled. "After the wedding you'll be together all the time. How are renovations going at the Richmond house?"

They chatted a little about Charlotte's plans for a nursery, and then Charlotte changed the subject. "So, about Burke."

Bella's body heated just at the sound of his name. "What about him?"

"He watches you a lot. I think he's interested."

She met Charlotte's gaze. They never really talked about the accident anymore. Bella had made it clear she didn't want to, but maybe that had been a mistake. It had happened. She couldn't just pretend that it didn't.

"He feels responsible for the accident, that's all. We've never talked about it."

"Not once? He's Will's best friend. How have you avoided him?"

"With great care and planning," Bella admitted.

One of the staff placed a glass of white wine in front of her and she was grateful for it. She took a fortifying sip and then put the glass down. "He…" She couldn't look at her sister right now, not as she said the words. "He found me in the pool the other night, after everyone had gone to bed. He saw my scars."

Charlotte put her hand over Bella's. "I'm sorry. I know how much care you take."

Bella turned her head to stare at her sister. "I do. And sometimes I wonder if I'm wrong to do so, but the thought—" She halted. The thought of her scars being out there for the world to see, to gawk at…she just couldn't.

"I know, sweetie. Still, it hurts to see you hide so much. You're a beautiful woman. But this is your life and your choice to live it how you want. What happened with Burke?"

"He was horrified," Bella admitted. "And why

wouldn't he be? Add that on to the trauma of the accident itself and it wasn't really a fun time. I didn't know he felt responsible, though. That's ridiculous."

"Why?" Charlotte sat back, took a sip of water and sent Bella a probing glance. "All of you made the choice to get in the car with Royce that night. Maybe Burke wishes he'd found a way to stop it instead."

"That's what he said."

"Seems to me he didn't come out of it unscathed, either. Just something to think about."

Bella pondered that for a while, sipping on the wine. "You're right, you know. But I still come back to the fact that the consequences for me are far more visible. I don't want to be looked at like some freak."

Charlotte leaned forward and squeezed Bella's hand. "Bella, you are not a freak," she said firmly. "You are one of the smartest people I've ever known, and wise, too. You give excellent advice. But it seems you aren't nearly as kind to yourself as you are to others."

That tidbit of insight from her little sister hit her deep inside. Was it true? Did she sabotage herself, talk down to herself? She'd never thought of it that way, but now that Charlotte had said it, Bella knew that she was harder on herself than anyone else was. Maybe to make up for what she'd put the family through.

She was going to answer Charlotte, but Gabi and Giulia appeared, and Gabi was so radiant as the bride-to-be that Bella put all heavier thoughts aside. Tonight was to celebrate and have fun, and she wouldn't spoil it with her maudlin thoughts.

Once they were all together, the staff member in charge of their spa selections, Maria, rounded them up to get started on their itinerary. They were given plush robes to change into, and Bella watched with envy as Giulia and Charlotte went for stone massages and Gabi chose a detoxifying body wrap. But to do any of those things would mean revealing her scars, and the last thing she needed was some tabloid picking up the news and running with it. Instead she chose the sauna, with essential oils in the steam to help her relax.

An hour later, they met for facials. Bella held her breath as the aesthetician put a band around her face to hold her hair back and then began her work on Bella's skin. She rarely let anyone see her without makeup; the white scars were smaller than other places on her body and there weren't as many, but they were still very visible without the right cosmetic coverage. But the woman said nothing about it, just smiled pleasantly and treated Bella's face to a myriad of delicious-smelling treatments. Bella let out a breath and consciously relaxed her body. It had been too long since she'd treated herself to something like this.

The women were quiet during the facials, but then the happy chatter began as they were served prosecco while soaking their feet in preparation for full pedicures. The bubbly wine was excellent and so was the company. Bella's throat tightened as she realized she hadn't had this kind of girls' day out in possibly forever. Had she really closed herself off so much that she had no friends?

She'd told herself family was enough. But was it? William was being married day after tomorrow. Charlotte was married and a baby would be coming before Christmas. When they all had their own families, where would she be? Alone? Spinster Tante Bella?

"Bel, are you all right?" Charlotte asked. "You've gone quiet."

"Actually," Bella replied, shaking away the depressing thoughts, "I was just thinking what a wonderful time this is. Not just the spa, but the four of us, together. I'm so glad we decided to do it."

She reached over and touched Gabi's arm. "And I'm very glad you're finally joining the family, Gabi."

"Aw, don't make me cry!" Gabi flapped her hands in front of her face.

Giulia grinned widely and lifted an eyebrow. "Someone get my sister more prosecco." They all laughed at that, and toasted when glasses were refilled. The mood lightened even more as their feet were buffed and nails painted, and then the same treatment was given to their hands. By the time it was all over, it was after seven and time for the scrumptious dinner that had been prepared for them by a renowned chef.

Bella went to bed that night with a heart full of love and camaraderie, but as she drifted off to sleep, she found herself wondering what else she'd missed out on all these years, and if it was worth it.

# CHAPTER FOUR

THE WEATHER WAS picture-perfect for Gabi and William's wedding, and to Bella's relief, the sweltering heat cooled slightly to a very pleasurable temperature. The wedding was taking place right at the villa, and yesterday and today had been nothing but bedlam as crews set up an arch of stunning pale pink and white roses in the courtyard, and then arranged pristine white chairs for the guests. With the forecast completely clear, caterers set up tables in the back garden, with full linens. Soon they'd add centerpieces of hydrangeas cut from Signora Baresi's own shrubs.

Inside, Bella tried to relax as the hairdresser they'd hired to come to the villa tamed her thick curls. With deft hands, the woman pulled some of the hair off Bella's face, pinning it in place with waxy gardenias, leaving the rest to trail down her back in artfully arranged curls. When she was done, she moved on to Giulia and then the bride.

Bella had offered to do everyone's makeup. After all, she managed the Aurora Cosmetics arm and she was quite adept. Her own routine was long but fairly straightforward, and the look was supposed to be summery and fresh, so she went ahead and did hers first, then went to Charlotte.

She ran into Burke in the hall.

He looked absolutely gorgeous. Dashing. Like a movie star. Her tongue tangled in her mouth as she stared at him, already in his tux, smelling like heaven. "You're ready."

"William's a bit of a wreck. I figured if I'm ready early, it'll be one less thing for him to stress over." He patted his pocket. "I was going to make a joke about the ring, but I'm not sure his heart could take it."

She laughed a little, self-conscious because she was still in her robe. "Well, you're the right doctor, in any case."

"I suppose so. Still, better not chance it. How was your hen night in Tuscany?"

"Amazing. And yours?"

"Very James Bond. Tuxedos, martinis, casinos. But we behaved ourselves."

She laughed. His twinkling eyes said they'd had fun regardless, and she wasn't sure she needed to know any details.

"I need to go. I'm doing the makeup, you see."

"You look beautiful."

She was sure she blushed. "I'm not even dressed yet."

His dark gaze held hers. "Doesn't matter. Anyway, see you down there."

He jogged off, his shiny shoes tapping on the floors, while she stared after him. Did he realize how casually he threw out compliments? She shouldn't take them to heart or get used to it. It was all part of the Burke Phillips charm, wasn't it?

She went to Charlotte's room to do her makeup, and then on to Gabi's room, where Giulia and Gabi waited. Giulia's hair was already done, and in a similar style to Bella's, though Giulia's hair was a little lighter and shorter. Gabi was sitting patiently while the hairdresser fixed her hair in loose waves and then pinned it back, creating a romantic look that would knock William off his feet. Bella went to work with her wands and brushes and sponges and before long the sisters were contoured and polished, lips glistening and eyes popping. "All that's left is your dresses," Bella said.

All the dresses were Aurora designs, including the wedding gown. Giulia put hers on first, and Bella zipped up the back. "Oh, to be twenty-three again," she murmured, as the zip slid smoothly to the top. The dress fit perfectly on Giulia's youthful figure.

"Oh, don't be silly." Giulia spun around and tut-tutted. "You're thirty. And have a body like a goddess."

"That's a lie, but thank you." Bella grinned. "Now for the bride." Charlotte had joined them, bringing the bouquets, and it was a sweet moment where they all came together to help Gabi into her dress. The column eased over her curves and fit perfectly on her shoulders. It was absolutely stunning. A classic design suited to a garden wedding. Signora Baresi came in and started to cry when she saw her daughter ready to walk down the aisle. "The final thing," she announced, and put a white box down on the bed. From it she took the veil, holding the gossamer length over her arm as she went to Gabi. The hairdresser helped anchor it so it was firmly in place without messing up Gabi's hairdo.

"My something old," she said, blinking quickly. "I'm not going to cry, but thank you, Mama. I'm so honored to wear your veil today."

Bella stepped forward. "In keeping with that tradition, my mother has offered you something borrowed." She reached into her robe pocket and took out a box holding a pair of diamond teardrop earrings. "These belonged to my great-grandmother, given to her by my great-grandfather, the sixth Earl of Chatsworth, on their wedding day."

"I lied. I might actually cry," Gabi said as she took the earrings from Bella.

"And something blue." This from Charlotte. It was a tiny blue crystal butterfly, which she tucked in among the delicate blossoms in Gabi's bouquet of freesias, white roses, and pale pink bouvardia.

There was a bunch of sniffling in the room, and then laughter.

A knock on the door had them all turning their heads. Stephen poked his head inside and zeroed in on Bella. "Bel, could I borrow you for a moment?"

"Sure." She still had to put on her dress, but otherwise she was ready and she could dress in a few minutes.

Once outside, Stephen's relaxed face tightened. "Sorry. It's Maman. She's not feeling well, and Burke is concerned."

Something dark settled in the pit of Bella's stomach as she hurried down the corridor behind him. They went into the library, where Aurora was seated in a chair, her feet up, William hovering nearby and Burke checking her pulse.

"Maman." She went to her mother and dropped a kiss on her forehead, not caring about leaving a lipstick mark. "What's wrong?"

"Nothing, but Viscount Downham is determined I go to the hospital." Bella knew her mother was annoyed when she started using titles.

"It's not nothing." Burke looked up at Bella. "She won't listen to me."

Aurora sighed. "I'm fine now. It doesn't hurt anymore. And this is William's wedding day."

William stopped pacing and stared at his mother. "Maman. I have waited for this day for what feels like forever, but not at your expense." No one mentioned their father's sudden cardiac death, but Bella was sure it was on all their minds.

Burke let go of Aurora's wrist. "I don't have any nitroglycerin with me, and I suspect it might be angina, but without tests we can't be sure."

"Sure of…?" asked Bella.

"If she's had a small heart attack or not."

Aurora flapped her hand, moved to get up, and at a stern look from Stephen, sat back in the chair. "I get these pains sometimes, but they don't last long. Just a bit, I don't know, squeezy."

"And how often has this been happening?" Bella moved to sit on the footstool before her mother, and her alarm grew when Aurora evaded her eyes.

Bella looked at Burke. "This is your call." His eyes widened, as if surprised she'd say such a thing. "Burke, you're a cardiologist. There's no one more qualified, and I trust you with this."

His throat bobbed when he swallowed, and he looked at Aurora. "I still think you need to go to the hospital. Perugia isn't that far. I can take you—"

"I'm not missing this wedding."

He sighed. "If I let you attend the wedding, will you promise me that if the pain comes back we go?" He looked her dead in the eyes. "I don't want to scare you, but statistically heart attacks are more devastating in women. Do you understand what I'm saying? And that *would* ruin Will's wedding."

"Maman," Will said, squatting down before her. "We can't lose you, too."

She sighed. "Darlings, you won't. Yes, Burke, I promise I will tell you if the pain comes back. And I will go to the hospital for tests tomorrow first thing if that's what you want."

"I do," Burke said, his gaze serious. "Even if it is angina, you need to know and get started on a treatment plan. I'll call ahead to set everything up."

"Thank you."

"In the meantime, you can attend the wedding but you must not exert yourself. Lay off the bubbly and no dancing until we know what's happening. Okay?"

She rolled her eyes. "Do I have a choice?"

"No." That came from four voices, spoken in unison.

There was a tap at the door and Christophe looked in. "The officiant is looking for the groom. Is everything okay in here?"

Will stood and nodded. "Sort of. Stephen, you talk to Charlotte, okay?"

Stephen nodded. He and Will went to leave,

which just left Burke and Bella in the room with
Aurora. And Bella still had to get dressed.

"I'll stay with her," Burke said, without Bella
even asking. "And when it's time I'll escort her
to her seat." Burke looked at Aurora and winked.
"Sorry, Lady Pemberton, but I guess you're stuck
with me as your date for the evening."

Aurora laughed then, a rich sound with just a
bit of grit in it, a sound that Bella loved to hear.
"All the ladies will have their noses out of shape,
I fear."

"They'll deal with the disappointment," he replied. Then he looked at Bella. "It's okay. Promise."

His warm assurance sent something soft and
fragile into Bella's heart, something she hadn't
let in there for a very long time. It was faith that
what he said was true, and a level of trust that
was foreign to her. She only had one parent left,
but she trusted Burke to make sure everything
was all right. How could that be?

"Thank you," she said, and touched his shoulder with her fingertips before leaving the room.
She had to get dressed. She had to walk down
the aisle as a bridesmaid. And she had to figure
out what to do about these feelings that were
cropping up every time Burke was around. If
she wasn't careful, she'd start to hope, and she
was very sure that the subsequent fall wouldn't
be worth it.

* * *

Burke left Aurora in her seat as mother of the groom and went to stand with William at the bower of roses. Stephen joined him at the front, and then Marco escorted Signora Baresi to her seat. The woman was beaming as she sat and waited for her husband to walk Gabi down the grassy aisle.

Nearly two hundred guests were in attendance, a huge crowd for the lovely but modest villa. Massimo Baresi was a successful man, and from what William had said, offered to host the wedding wherever they wanted. Massimo was also a cancer survivor, and William had told Burke that what Gabi really wanted was for her father to escort her to her groom at the villa they called home. So...the venue was brought to them. Burke had to admit it was beautiful. The sun was shining, birds were singing, and there were flowers everywhere.

Violins began playing something vaguely familiar, and Burke's attention was diverted to the arch in the courtyard where the bridesmaids waited. First came Charlotte, with her pregnant glow and a just-discernible bubble where she was starting to show. A quick glance at Jacob told Burke that the Big Viking, as he now called him, was utterly smitten.

Then Bella. Burke's breath caught as she stepped out, her powder-blue dress flowing around her ankles. The light fabric covered her arms and her hair was down, and now he knew why. It didn't make her any less beautiful. This morning, when she'd said she trusted him with her mother—that had been so unexpected. She had no reason to trust his judgment, did she? He'd made his share of mistakes. But there'd been no question in her eyes, no doubt. She'd put her faith in him to care for one of the dearest people in her life.

Of course, people did that every day in his line of work, and it wasn't something he took lightly. But for Bella to do so…was different.

She got closer, holding her bouquet and smiling, and then her gaze slid to his and her smile wobbled a little as that annoying *zing* ran between them, a current that was getting harder and harder to ignore.

Once upon a time she'd tried to get his attention and he'd ignored her. And for good reason. Now, though, he seemed unable to look away.

Giulia followed behind, and Burke noticed that Marco couldn't take his eyes off her. A smile touched his lips. They were so young and in love.

And finally, there was Gabi, on her father's arm, looking radiant in her dress with a veil that trailed behind her. Burke heard William's sharp intake of breath, and he looked over at his friend to see Will's lower lip wobbling. Who would have ever thought that his best friend would be hit so hard by love? Marriage…and probably a family, too. And here was Burke, two years older, and matrimony and babies weren't anywhere near his radar.

And then he looked and saw Bella lift a tissue to her eyes and it changed everything.

He was interested in the one woman who truly wanted nothing to do with him. Wasn't that just his luck? And even if she were interested, Bella wasn't the kind of woman he could flirt with, or have a fling with, as attractive as that idea may be. He was not his father's son. He wouldn't treat someone so special so…cavalierly. He'd kept his relationships—using that term loosely—at a surface level, charming and pleasant but never deeper. He never, ever wanted to be responsible for hurting someone the way his father had by his actions. Added to that, Bella was different. It could never be just easy and light with her because of their shared trauma. They were already bonded in a much deeper way.

His gaze shifted to Aurora, sitting in the front row with Christophe and Jacob. She smiled up at him and gave a slight nod. Good. He'd be watching her like a hawk all day. Better to put his focus there than on Bella. Easier said than done.

The ceremony commenced and when the time came for the ring, Burke reached into his pocket and took out the diamond-studded wedding band. He watched as his best friend made his vows and slid the ring over Gabi's finger, his heart catching when she said the vows back, tears hovering on her lids, and put a ring on William's finger, too. Gabi truly, truly loved him. The way Aurora had loved Cedric, he realized. Of course he wanted that for his friend. Something steadfast and loyal. Unlike his own parents' union.

No one had ever looked at him that way, though. And he wasn't sure he wanted them to. This past week was not representative of his life. He pulled long hours at the hospital, did his share of night and weekend on calls. And his career wasn't going to stagnate here. There was so much to learn, places he could go. He wasn't sure how a relationship would fit into that. He'd seen what happened when a husband was more dedicated to his work than his wife. That was not a legacy he ever wanted to continue.

The ceremony ended with Will and Gabi kissing and then beaming so brightly they nearly put the sun to shame. As they retreated down the aisle, Burke offered his arm to Giulia, while Stephen escorted Bella, and Marco, Charlotte. Soon they were in the flower garden, where the couple would receive congratulations, and Burke moved off to the side, eager to check on Aurora.

Bella came to his side. "I want to check on Maman."

"Me as well. Here she comes." He stepped forward and offered Aurora a kiss on the cheek. "Well, he's all married up now," Burke teased, checking her face for any signs of strain or pain. "Feeling all right? Any dizziness or weakness?"

"Just a little tired." Aurora smiled at him. "See? I'm being honest." Her gaze locked with his. "I promise I'm taking this seriously, Burke. The timing was just…"

He touched her elbow. "You should have had it looked at before now. You must take care of yourself, you know."

She nodded. "I know."

Bella was standing by Burke's shoulder. "Would you like something cool to drink, Maman?"

"That would be lovely, Bella, thank you."

When Bella was gone, Burke stared into Aurora's eyes. "Losing Cedric was hard on your children. I would imagine they are afraid of losing another parent. Even grown children flounder when they lose their anchor, Aurora."

Her lip quivered but only for the briefest moment. He saw it and pretended not to. His message had sunk in.

"And you would know, too. I'm sorry about your father. He and Cedric were good friends."

"Cedric was a good man. Better than I can hope to be," Burke replied.

They moved into the shade and Burke found Aurora a chair so she could rest. "Why do you say that, and not include your father?" she asked, peering up at him. "Your father was very proud of you."

"You know why."

"Ah, yes. The accident."

She was only partly right, and he wasn't about to elaborate. What good would it do now? Not one bit. If Aurora didn't know about his father's indiscretions, then maybe the previous viscount had been more discreet than Burke had given him credit for. He shifted the topic slightly. "I didn't know about Bella. Being so injured. Not until this week."

"She wanted it that way."

"So William said."

"And with you all being minors except Royce, we were able to keep your names out of it. You were foolish teenagers. And you've all paid a heavy price for that."

"Have I?" He looked down at her sharply. "My life looks pretty good, doesn't it?"

Aurora held his gaze. "What we see on the outside and what's on the inside don't often match up. I'd say you've paid more than you want to let on. Including taking on much of the guilt and responsibility."

"Because it's right. I do have responsibility."

He could see Bella returning and knew they would have to change the subject. But Aurora got in one last thought. "Maybe so. Even if you do, though, it doesn't make the burden any easier to bear."

He thought about her words as Bella handed her mother a glass of punch and they spoke for a few moments about the wedding. Oddly enough, he'd found Aurora's words comforting. She didn't try to convince him his feelings were wrong. She simply acknowledged them. Funny how that made him feel better.

They spent the next hour mingling and then posing for photos. As the afternoon waned, they joined the guests in the garden for cocktails and charcuterie, and then finally a sit-down dinner of stuffed lamb leg and seasonal vegetables that was to die for. Wine flowed and a traditional Italian wedding cake was served with more prosecco. Burke and Bella sat at the same table as the bride and groom, though not beside each other. Still, he seemed attuned to her every laugh and smile. When the dancing finally started beneath sparkling lights, Burke checked on Aurora. She danced once with William as Gabi danced with her father, and then dutifully went back to her seat, watching the festivities.

Today had scared her. He was glad of it. It would make his job tomorrow much easier.

And after he danced with Giulia, he held out his hand to Bella. "Dance?" he asked, trying to keep his voice casual.

"Oh, I…uh…"

"Can't think of a decent excuse?" He laughed. "I promise I'll behave."

She rolled her eyes. "Don't make promises you can't keep."

He left his hand in the air between them. "One dance," he said.

She relented and put her fingers in his, and they walked to the dance floor that had been installed for the occasion. He took her in his arms, one hand clasping hers, the other on the soft material of her dress. "In case I didn't tell you today," he murmured in her ear, "you look beautiful."

"You did tell me," she murmured, her feet shuffling to the music. "In the hall."

"Right. And then you put on the dress, and… just wow, Bella."

She leaned back and looked in his face. "I don't need your compliments."

"Maybe I want to give them just the same." She felt good in his arms, almost like she belonged there. "You know, I was a fool all those years ago."

She lifted an eyebrow. "We both were."

"You were flirting with me that night. And I ignored you."

Her chin came up. "Me? Flirting? You mean you were walking around as if you were God's gift to women!"

Now, wasn't that an interesting reaction. Had he perhaps hit a nerve?

"Well, I was. Acting that way," he clarified. "Not that I actually was, as you say, 'God's gift to women.' But I noticed you, Bella. I just wanted you to know that."

Her gaze locked on his, and he didn't see the anger he expected. Instead he saw confusion and what he thought might be…regret? Or was that just him projecting his own feelings on her?

"Then why?" she asked. "Why did you treat me as if I were invisible?"

# CHAPTER FIVE

BELLA COULD HAVE kicked herself for asking. Burke was so handsome, so charming, and the way he'd cared for her mother today…good heavens, he was nearly perfect. It only ended up making Bella feel more flawed. And forgettable.

Oh, the irony. Because she tried to fly under the radar at the best of times. Still, when it came to wanting a guy to notice you, complete indifference was a tough pill to swallow.

He sighed, and when she met his gaze she saw nothing but honesty in the depths. "I did that because your brothers told me to keep my hands to myself. No messing around with you or Charlotte."

Her mouth dropped open. Not in a million years had she expected that sort of answer. "They did what?"

"Before the party. We're the same age, Bella, and I happened to say to Stephen that I thought you were quite beautiful. I believe his response was, 'She's my sister and she's off-limits.'"

I wasn't about to argue. Have you seen your brother? He and the Big Viking make a smaller man think twice about crossing them."

Their feet kept moving to the music, but Bella's brain was awhirl. This was news that her brothers had never shared with her.

"But you…oh, never mind." What did it matter? At least this explained a lot. But it also made her a little bit angry. If he hadn't been so cold to her, she wouldn't have sought out Royce to make Burke jealous. It had worked, too. Burke and the girl he'd latched on to, some girl that Stephen knew, had agreed to go with them to Royce's estate to raid his father's liquor cabinet. It had all seemed so daring and exciting in the moment. And remarkably irresponsible and stupid.

"Bella." The song ended and he let go of her hand. "Can we please talk about this later? Really talk about it? We both have feelings about that night that need airing. Otherwise we're still stuck there, don't you see? Don't you want to be able to let it go?"

"We'll see," she said, taking a step back. She'd gone to pains to avoid him all week, but the truth was with so many people around, it was nearly impossible to get any time alone. She was coming around to the conclusion that he was right. They did need to talk about it. He had been there. He knew. And for all Bella's assertions over the years, she hadn't moved on. She was stuck, just as he said.

"I'm going to check on Maman," she said, turning away.

He fell into step beside her. "Why don't you come with us tomorrow?"

"To the hospital, you mean?"

He nodded. "I think your mother would like to have a family member there. And that maybe a daughter might be a bit gentler than Stephen's… shall we say, autocratic tendencies?"

She laughed then. "I know you're best friends with Will, but that was very accurate."

"I can usually read people. The fact that I can't figure you out is really bothering me."

She laughed again. "Well, at least I'm not predictable." They'd reached Aurora's side and Bella took the chair next to her. "Well, Maman, what do you think?"

"I think this was a beautiful wedding, and that I'm very proud of all my children." She smiled warmly. "All of them." And she reached for Bella's hand.

"Thank you."

"I know how hard you work, Bella. I see everything." She looked up at Burke. "I'm sure you understand those workaholic tendencies, too, yes? I imagine your schedule is a full one."

"No one goes into medicine for the great hours," he replied.

"And Isabel? She's managing all right?" she inquired after his mother.

"She is." Burke sat down beside Bella. "One of my sisters got married last year. The other one is working in London so still staying in the house. Mother says that once Josey leaves, she's not sure what she'll do with all that space."

"Fill it with grandchildren?"

He laughed. "She'll have to rely on my sisters for that, I'm afraid."

A faster song came on and one of the guests came to snag Burke, who shrugged and let himself be led away. Bella leaned back in her chair and watched as Burke moved smoothly on the floor, natural rhythm taking over the movement of his body...particularly his hips. Bella jumped a little when Aurora started laughing.

"Oh, sweetheart, you are so transparent. If you want him, go get him."

"What? No. I don't...no." She dragged her gaze away from the sight of him and faced her mother. "We're barely friendly."

"You've started talking about what happened."

"A little."

"And you trust him."

She sighed. She couldn't deny that part because people had witnessed her saying it. "I trust his judgment as a doctor," she replied carefully.

"And he's very good-looking."

"I'm not blind."

Aurora lifted her glass to her lips, then lowered it. "You could do worse, Bella. Burke Phillips is a good man."

"I have no desire to be Lady Downham." Which wasn't strictly true. Not that she wanted to marry him or anything, but the barely friendly bit had been inaccurate. They were speaking more than they ever had, but it was what they weren't saying that drew her in. And she was ridiculously attracted to him. That hadn't changed, from the time she was a teenager until now, a grown woman with her own busy life to manage.

"Keep an open mind," Aurora suggested. "You can't quite fit love into convenient little boxes."

Bella frowned. What was that supposed to mean? But before she could ask, Marco claimed her for a dance, and she went on to enjoy the rest of the wedding.

Everything was subdued the next morning. The bride and groom had driven to Perugia last night, to spend their wedding night in a hotel suite before leaving on their honeymoon the following evening. Bella was awake early, and a careful listen told her no one else in the house was up yet. She stretched, sighed, and got up to shower.

She was going to the hospital with Burke and her mother today. They'd settled it last night. Burke would be by at nine, they'd drive into the city, and hopefully be back in time for dinner.

He'd been right about her mother not being alone today. Burke was kind but he wasn't family. And Charlotte did deserve to spend the morning with her husband, whom she'd barely seen since his arrival.

She just had to figure out how to stem the uneasiness that gripped her every time she thought about her mother being ill. It seemed like yesterday they'd lost Cedric. Aurora was now the captain of the ship. What was Aurora Inc. without her? A ship without a captain…or maybe a ship without a rudder, if she took the metaphor a little further. There simply was no Aurora Inc. without Maman at the helm.

The shower felt heavenly and she dressed quickly, in jeans and a light peasant-style shirt that would be comfortable for sitting in a waiting room. She dressed up the ensemble with a pair of melon-colored heels and a turquoise necklace, the pops of color transforming her simple outfit into something more.

Then there was her hair and makeup to consider. It took nearly an hour for her to dry and style the heavy mass, and then another twenty-five minutes for makeup. What would it be like to shove her hair in a messy topknot and go out with nothing more than a swipe of lip gloss and mascara? Sometimes she really didn't enjoy being high maintenance.

When she was finally ready, she slipped her

small laptop into her bag. No reason why she couldn't distract herself with some work. Charlotte had agreed to cover William's teams while he was honeymooning, at least. But Bella knew that Charlotte was only one person. And with Maman not feeling well, keeping an eye on the company as a whole wasn't a bad idea. She paused at her doorway. Maybe what she needed to do was schedule a meeting with Stephen when they returned to Paris. Between the two of them, they should be able to carry the load so Maman could rest. Christophe, too, could be utilized in areas other than his jewelry division.

Aurora was already in the kitchen with Signora Baresi. "*Buongiorno*, Bella," said Lucia. "Would you like some breakfast?"

"I don't want you to go to any trouble. You must be exhausted after the last week."

"*Si*, but for the best reasons. Yesterday was so lovely." She put a cup of tea at Bella's elbow. "The *alla menta, si?*"

"*Grazie*," Bella replied, the soothing aroma of her customary mint tea touching her nostrils. "This is perfect."

A plate of bread and butter and jam appeared. Bella fixed a slice and began to eat; she wasn't sure what the day would bring and this light meal would hold her until they had a better idea.

"Maman, you're not eating?"

"No. I don't know if I need to fast for any

bloodwork, so I'm going to wait." She said it all very calmly, but Bella looked over and saw a tiny knit in one of her mother's usually flawless eyebrows. She was worried. And when Maman was particularly stressed, her appetite suffered. She might be right about the bloodwork, but it was also a convenient excuse.

Burke arrived and before long they were on the road to Perugia. Forty-five minutes would get them from the villa to the hospital. Once there, they took their time getting Aurora registered and the paperwork sorted. Then they sat to wait. It didn't take long. Burke had called ahead to an old acquaintance he had in the cardiology department. Bella went into the room with Burke and her mother during the initial exam, and sat with her while blood was taken. She moved to the side and waited quietly while Aurora was hooked up to an EKG machine, which made a quiet hum as it began to print out the pattern of her heartbeat.

Burke had a look at the tape when the nurse stepped out, but Bella couldn't read his face at all. He was in doctor mode now, wasn't he? The way he'd greeted his friend and then started talking…she really started to understand that he was no longer a boy but a man, and a very successful and smart man at that. There was a gravitas to him in this setting that she'd overlooked in the celebratory setting of the wedding. He inspired confidence and calm. It was quite remarkable, when all was said and done.

When it was time for the chest X-ray, Bella went back to the waiting room. Despite the excellent care, it still felt as if a heavy weight were just waiting to drop on the Pemberton family again. She swallowed around the lump in her throat and dug into her bag for her laptop. The less Maman had to worry about right now, the better.

It felt like a very long time before Burke joined her again. "Bella. Your mother is nearly finished. Do you want to come back in?"

She nodded, closing the lid on the laptop. Her chest tightened and as if he sensed her nervousness, Burke reached down and took her hand. He led her down a different hallway now, to an office, where Aurora waited, her face pale.

Burke and Bella went in and sat, and were immediately followed by the doctor, who smiled and took his seat behind his desk.

"Signora Pemberton, you did not have a heart attack." He smiled at her reassuringly. "This is very good news. Your bloodwork did not show any of the enzymes we would expect to see in that case, and your chest X-ray was normal as well."

Bella let out her breath in a rush, and Aurora visibly relaxed.

"Your EKGs did show a few abnormalities," he continued. "Your resting EKG seemed very normal, but we did notice a few things on the exercise EKG that I feel require further investigation. After talking with Dr. Phillips, I'm going to recommend you see a doctor in either Paris or London for an angiogram to look for artery blockages, and treatment from there. In addition, I'm giving you a prescription for nitroglycerin in case of another event."

"An angiogram…" Aurora said, her voice a little thready. "What would happen after that?"

Burke nodded at the doctor and then turned his attention to Aurora. "Well, quite often we'll do an angioplasty right there in the cath lab if we find a blockage. That's the little balloon procedure you've probably heard about. Sometimes we put in a stent at the same time. Depending on the blockage, sometimes a bypass operation is recommended. But let's not put the cart before the horse."

"Dr. Phillips is right. Take it easy, eat well, get rest. The angiogram should tell you more. We could schedule you in here, but since you've said your time in Italy is coming to a close, and considering today's results, waiting for you to reach home would be fine, in my opinion."

Bella felt a rush of relief sweep over her. This didn't sound great, but it certainly could sound a lot worse.

The doctor wrote out two prescriptions and handed them to Aurora. "One is for the nitro. The other is for a daily medication. Your cardiologist at home may change that depending on his diagnosis. Do you have a cardiologist?"

"I have Dr. Phillips," Aurora said firmly.

"Aurora, I try not to treat friends and family. Though I appreciate your confidence immensely."

She nodded. "Well, you're my doctor until we can go back, and you can recommend someone to me."

"That I can do, and happily."

They rose and shook the doctor's hand before leaving the office and finding their way back outside to where Burke had parked.

He'd closed the door after Aurora had slipped into the back seat, and Bella looked at him over the roof of the car. "I don't know the city, but I can tell you Maman hasn't eaten all day. She was too nervous this morning. Could we find somewhere to grab a bite? It's a long time until dinner." They'd missed the lunch hour and it was now half past two.

"Of course. I can check my phone and find someplace close."

He moved to get into the car but she stopped him again, keeping her voice low so Aurora couldn't hear. "Thank you. For what you did for Maman yesterday and for taking care of this today. It means a lot, Burke."

It was hard to say that to him. It shouldn't have

been, for it was simple gratitude and appreciation. But it was, just the same. Because things were not simple between them, as much as she might like them to be.

"It's what I do," he answered plainly. "I would do it for anyone."

They got in the car and Bella shut the door. She doubted he would understand, but his last statement only made her respect and like him more. Because she knew it was true. He'd take the same care with any person, and that said a lot about him as a human being.

It was getting harder and harder not to like him more than was advisable.

# CHAPTER SIX

THE FOLLOWING DAY the Pemberton crew said goodbye to the Baresis, thanking them for their hospitality, and boarded a chartered jet to Paris and then London. Charlotte, Jacob, Christophe, and Stephen would be staying in Paris, and Bella was going on to London with Aurora and Burke. Aurora had an appointment with one of Burke's colleagues on Wednesday, and Burke had advised that she would be booked in for an angiogram. If she ended up having the balloon procedure, she would spend a night in hospital and then time off, recovering.

Bella had, without any formal decision, become the child to be at Aurora's side. She wasn't sure why.

Once on the plane, however, Aurora made an announcement. She held a family meeting—minus William—about what would happen with Aurora Inc. as she dealt with her illness.

She looked at Charlotte first. "Charlotte, you've already got your hands full with public relations and handling William's division while he's away. Plus you're growing another human." She smiled warmly. "I'd like your plans to remain unchanged."

"I agree," Charlotte replied, putting her hand on her tummy. "I'm trying to be very good about balancing work and rest. But if you need something, you know you must call."

"I know, darling, and I will." Aurora turned her attention to Christophe. "Christophe, I'm adding to your workload a little bit. I want you to work with Bella to take over some of her responsibilities on an interim basis. She can decide what to hand off to you and what she can delegate within her division."

"Yes, Aunt." Christophe looked at Bella. "If you're going on to London, I'll make myself available for a virtual meeting whenever you need, Bel."

"Maman, I know I'm coming with you, but I can keep up with my work." Bella frowned. Had she not kept everything going while they were in Italy? And she was fine! She wasn't overworked. It felt…punitive.

Aurora held Bella's gaze. "Of course, you can keep up with your work, but you can't do that and keep up with *my* work."

Bella's eyes widened.

"I'm going to take some time off to get my health under control. While I'm out of the office,

Bella is the new me." She looked around at all the children for affirmation.

Bella's mouth dropped open. She'd planned to talk to Stephen about helping, but she hadn't counted on officially being handed the reins. "Me? Not Stephen?"

Stephen spoke up. "I'm the numbers guy, Bel. I work with acquisitions and legal and all the dry business stuff. But Maman is right. She's the heart of Aurora, and you're the next best thing. Christophe can manage cosmetics with your help."

She looked around at Charlotte and Christophe. "And you're both all right with this?"

"Why wouldn't we be?" This was from Christophe. "Bel, you're the one who is always behind the scenes, holding us together. You are *la colle*."

Hah. She would hardly consider herself anyone's glue. She was still stunned by the announcement. "But Maman. I'm going to be in London with you."

"Only for a little while. It's the perfect way for me to debrief you on what you need to know moving forward. Then you can return to Paris and work out of my office, or yours. Whichever you're comfortable with. My assistant will be at your disposal."

Burke's voice came from behind her. "Congratulations, Bella."

Congratulations were echoed throughout the cabin.

Aurora addressed them all again. "I'm very proud of all my children. I know I've said that often lately, but it's true. You've all stepped up into your roles in the company and done a wonderful job. And covering for each other makes you versatile so you can understand the company as a whole. I'm not retiring yet, *mes petites*, but when I do, I know Aurora Inc. is in more than capable hands."

Bella blinked away a few tears, and she saw Charlotte do the same. Stephen reached over and squeezed Aurora's hand. She had the best family. Maybe they were all missing Cedric, but they still had one another and they were still strong.

When the conversation moved to other subjects, Bella got up and went to the galley to get a drink. She was pouring club soda into a glass when Burke came up behind her. "Well. I take it that was unexpected."

She put down the bottle and turned to face him. "Totally unexpected."

"You can do it, though."

"Hell yes, I can," she agreed, and was gratified when Burke burst out laughing. It did strike her, though, that she was going to be running—even on a temporary basis—a billion-dollar company. It was a huge enterprise consisting of fashion, cosmetics, jewelry. The only way to run it was to trust in the people below her. The way Maman had trusted in her.

"You're something, Bella, you know that?" They were tucked away in the little galley at the front of the plane, out of sight from the others, and he was close, so close. She looked up and saw his deep gaze probing hers, and she couldn't look away. His lips were getting closer, and then he did it…he touched his lips to hers, softly, and yet with a persuasiveness that wooed her into closing her eyes and melting against him just a little bit.

It was even better than she'd imagined.

He took his time, and Bella was in no rush, either. She couldn't remember the last time she'd been kissed, and the sensation was wonderful. Delicious. His lips were soft, and so was his beard as it brushed against her chin and cheeks. Mmm… She'd never kissed a man with a beard before, but she could get used to it.

And then she remembered that they were in a three-foot-by-three-foot section of airplane, barely hidden from her family, and she shifted back in the little room she had, breaking off the kiss and running her tongue along her lower lip, as if to savor every last taste of him. He made her feel things. Not just yearning, but a knowledge that this was a part of her life that she'd been deprived of exploring, and that brought resentment with it.

"Complicated," he said simply. He ran a finger over his bottom lip and held her gaze. "And I should probably apologize."

"No, don't," she said quickly. Perhaps too quickly. "I mean, there's nothing to apologize for. It was just a kiss. And we were both willing participants."

A slow smile crept up his cheeks, making a crease in his dimple that she could see even with the close-cropped facial hair. It would be hard for any woman to resist it. Even harder for her, because she was also starting to really admire the man inside the sexy package.

"I should get back," she added, and skirted him with her drink in hand.

Either the family hadn't noticed she and Burke had been in the galley or they were choosing to ignore it. Either way, she took her seat and then joined in the conversation, which had turned strategic. Never let it be said the Pembertons didn't know how to have a good time, she thought.

But strategy and work were her comfort zone, far more than sneaking into alcoves with sexy doctors. That was right up there with surprising midnight swims. She wasn't quite sure what to do in those situations, or how she was supposed to feel and act. Work, though, that was a familiar beast.

Maybe getting home and getting to work would help banish this restless feeling that had been plaguing her ever since she'd left for Italy. Getting back into regular habits and schedules would surely level things out.

* * *

They stopped in Paris and said goodbye to Christophe, Stephen, Jacob, and Charlotte. Then they took off again, headed to Gatwick as the drive from Gatwick to Chatsworth Manor wasn't difficult at all.

"Burke, you must come stay," Aurora said, tapping her nails on the arm rest of her seat. "It's been too long since you were at Chatsworth."

"That's kind, but I do have to be back at the hospital tomorrow morning. I'll be there on Wednesday, though. I won't be in on the procedure, but I'll be close by."

"You can keep Bella updated, then," Aurora said, looking pleased.

"Of course."

He looked over at Bella. "Where are you staying when you come to town?"

"I thought I would stay at Charlotte's," she replied. "Jacob's stayed in Paris with her and the house is empty."

"Charlotte's quite a distance from the hospital, though, isn't she? All the way over in Richmond."

Bella looked at Aurora and frowned. What was her mother getting at? If she was trying to play matchmaker, Bella wished she'd cease and desist. Especially since Aurora was wearing what her children liked to call her "innocent" face. It never worked because Aurora was always too on the ball to be oblivious to anything.

"Then I'll get a hotel," she answered, her voice firm. "Honestly, Mother. I'm pretty sure I can manage this."

"Of course you can." Burke backed her up. "And if all goes well, it'll only be for one night."

Bella was thankful that he hadn't suggested staying with him, as she was sure that was what Aurora was angling at. Not that it wasn't an alluring idea. But she and Burke had shared one stolen kiss. It was a big stretch to go from there to spending the night. At least, that was what she told herself.

They landed and it took no time at all for them to disembark. They walked through the airport together, where a car service was waiting for Aurora and Bella. Burke was going to take a taxi home. As they prepared to go their separate ways, Bella realized that even though the wedding week had been disconcerting in many ways, she was rather sorry it was over. Now it was back to real life. Or at least as real as it could be with Aurora's medical issues in the picture.

But as the driver stowed their bags, Bella turned to Burke and found that it was hard to say goodbye.

"I'll see you Wednesday," he said, his voice low. "I'll wait with you."

"You don't have to do that."

"I want to. Both for Aurora and for you, so you don't have to wait alone."

He was so caring. So considerate. Nothing at all like she'd expected or like he'd been before. "That's very kind."

Aurora had slipped into the back of the car and now was waiting for Bella, but Burke put his hand on her arm.

"The hell with kind." His voice was rough. "I want to see you again, Bella. Even if that's in a hospital waiting room. That's not kind, that's selfish."

Oh, those words were thrilling. She met his gaze and tried a saucy smile. "That's not selfish, it's efficient," she answered. "I'll see you Wednesday."

Then she slipped into the limo before she could say anything more. It was bad enough that her mother was getting ideas. If she wasn't careful she'd be getting them, too.

Flirting was one thing. But it would be folly to attempt to take this somewhere it was never meant to go. Burke was handsome and nice and she was insanely attracted. But their lives were too different for anything more.

"I got an update from Dr. Mallick. The angiogram shows a blockage, so they're going to do an angioplasty and put in a stent. It'll be a little while longer."

Bella looked up at Burke, both relief and fear making her chest tighten. "This is good, right? I mean, not that she needs it, but that they found it and can fix it."

"Yes, exactly." He smiled reassuringly. "It should only take another hour or so."

Bella nodded. They'd met Dr. Mallick earlier this morning and he'd put a lot of her fears to rest as he'd explained the catheterization procedure. Burke had been with them, and knowing he had full confidence in his colleague also helped a lot. As much as Bella wished it was Burke in there doing the procedure, she respected his ethics that kept him out of the catheterization lab. Plus, there was the bonus that he had promised to wait with her, keeping her company.

She'd brought work but couldn't concentrate, so Burke had taken her to the café in the north wing for breakfast. After tea and hot buttered toast, she felt much better. Burke had then regaled her with stories as he gave her a tour of the hospital. One look at his animated face told her he was happy here, in his chosen field. There was passion and dedication in his voice, and she admired him for it. Despite the privilege of his birth, he'd worked very hard to get here, and her admiration for him grew.

He squeezed her hand. "Do you have something to read? A silly computer game on your phone?" They sat down in the waiting room chairs again. "You should keep your mind busy with something so you're not worrying."

"I know I shouldn't worry. She's in good hands and this is a common procedure." She looked over at him, still holding his hand. "But I worry anyway."

"Because she's your mother. And because she's the only parent you have left. I understand, Bella, more than you know."

He'd lost his father, too. She leaned against him briefly. "I know you do."

"You must miss Cedric a lot. He was such a good man. You're a lot like him."

Bella turned to look at him. "I am? How?"

"Your father never needed the spotlight. I remember seeing him and how he was so happy to let your mother shine and he stayed in the background. But he was her anchor. You could tell by the way she looked at him. He was the strength behind everything. And while Stephen has gone on to be the next earl, I think you're the one in the background making sure everything is all right. It's why Aurora chose to put you in charge while she's absent. You don't need the spotlight. You don't want it. And not just because of your scars. Because of who you are."

She stared at him in astonishment. "That's quite an assessment, Burke." But inside, she was warmed by his confidence in her. She loved the idea of being like her father. He'd been a wonderful man and she missed him more than anyone knew. What Burke had given her just now was a gift. A lovely gift she could hold inside and keep close during the days when she felt most alone.

"I've talked to William, too, you know. He said how fair you were when he and Gabi first got together and the family found out. How everyone can count on you to be the voice of reason. You're appreciated, Bella, more than you realize."

The endorsements were wonderful, but something caught at Bella, too. It was true; she tried to be fair and reasonable and see things from all sides. Because she'd deliberately tried to stay out of the limelight, she'd become very good at observing and assessing. But she wondered, too, if all that reliability made her...boring. She'd never done anything impulsive since the accident, having learned her lesson all too well. She lived a glamorous life but stayed on the sidelines. Never any whiff of scandal. What did that say about her? She didn't think it was because she was above doing anything scandalous. She had a sneaky suspicion it was because she had stopped living her life.

"What's wrong?" She'd been quiet so long that Burke had begun to frown. "Did I say something?"

"No, it's not you. I've just been thinking a lot lately." She tried a smile. "Maybe I need to get out of my own head a bit."

The creases in his brow relaxed. "We all do, from time to time."

They waited in silence for a while, and then Dr. Mallick came through the doors with a smile on his face. Burke and Bella stood.

"All done," Dr. Mallick announced. "The procedure went well with no complications. Mrs. Pemberton will be taken to her room shortly, where she'll spend the night, but barring any changes, she can go home tomorrow. She's still sedated and it'll be a little while for that to wear off completely. She's a bit groggy now."

Relief sluiced through Bella. All morning she'd told herself this was a common procedure and there was nothing to worry about, but deep down her concern had been profound. It was as if a heavy weight had been lifted from her shoulders.

"Thank you. Thank you so much," she said, letting out a breath and smiling in return.

Burke shook Dr. Mallick's hand. "Yes, thanks." Bella listened with half an ear as they discussed which medications Aurora would be prescribed. All she could truly think was that her mother was all right. Ever since the angina attack, a pall had fallen over the family.

"Excuse me a moment," she said, touching Burke's arm. "I want to call Paris."

"Of course." Burke chatted with Dr. Mallick while she stepped away to make the call.

Stephen was on a conference call, so she was put through to Charlotte, who would then relay the news to the rest of the family. "Charlotte? It's Bella. Everything went fine. She had to have a stent put in, but she's all done now and just has to stay overnight."

Charlotte's voice echoed Bella's relief. "So quickly? I thought she was just having the test this morning."

"They found the blockage and put the stent in while she was already catheterized. Dr. Mallick made it sound easy." She shook her head. "I'm just so grateful."

"Me, too, Bel. Me, too. To lose Maman…"

The silence that fell on the call spoke volumes.

"How are you feeling? Baby all right?"

"The baby's fine. And I have something I want to talk to you about, but not right now. Later this week? Personal, not business. So nothing to worry about."

"That sounds great."

"And Burke? Is he there with you?"

Heat infused Bella's cheeks. "He's been here the whole time."

"He's a good man, Bel. And he's got a thing for you."

"Don't be silly. He's a friend to the family." Not strictly true, of course.

"I know he kissed you on the plane. Why else were you in the galley for so long?"

Bella choked on a laugh. "We were discussing club soda."

"Sure you were." And Charlotte laughed back. "I'm just saying, don't turn down a great possibility because of…well, you know. I don't think Burke would care at all."

It wasn't about Burke caring. It was about her allowing herself to be so vulnerable. She didn't know if she could do it.

She looked over at him and he caught her eye and smiled. His eyes crinkled at the corners and his gaze was so warm she went melty. "I appreciate the advice," she replied.

"I doubt it, but I'm offering it anyway."

"Because you do speak your mind. Most of the time."

"When it comes to other people. Not so much when it comes to myself. But I'm getting better at it." Charlotte had tried so hard to toe the Aurora line that she'd almost lost herself in the process. Jacob had changed all that, and now Charlotte was really coming into her own. It had been good for her and for the company.

"I need to go, but you'll let everyone else know? Do you want me to text William? I know he's checking for updates, even though he and Gabi are still on their honeymoon."

"That'd be great, and I'll talk to Stephen and Christophe."

"Perfect. Love you, Charlotte."

"I love you, too, Bel."

Bella hung up with a lump in her throat. As a

family their love was always assured but rarely spoken. But today, as in many days since their father's death, it felt important to articulate it. They didn't say "I love you" enough.

She took a few more moments to fire off a text to William, then looked up to find Burke waiting for her where she'd left him. Dr. Mallick was gone, and now it was just the two of them.

"All set?" he asked.

She nodded. "I've called Charlotte and texted William. Charlotte will do the rest. When do you think I can see her?"

"Soon. But she'll probably sleep for a while. Why don't we find lunch somewhere?"

"You don't have to stay," she said, tucking her phone into her bag again. "You've done so much already."

"Bella." He took her hand. "Does it look like I want to be anywhere else?"

He had to stop saying things like that. She'd soon start believing him.

"Well, I could do with lunch. Something more than tea and toast." She smiled up at him.

"How do you feel about sushi?"

"It sounds perfect."

They made their way outside. The drizzly morning had made way for a brighter afternoon, with sun and a few spots of cloud. The restaurant was situated in a hotel that was literally steps from the hospital. Burke held the door for her as they went inside. "It's so close. Do you eat here often?"

"Yes and no. If I'm grabbing lunch on shift, sometimes I don't leave the hospital. Or there's a noodle takeaway not far that's decent and fast."

"No need for five-star dining?"

He laughed. "Hardly. Some days I pack a peanut butter sandwich for myself. I can cook, you know."

She was trying to picture that as they were shown to a table. They both ordered still water to drink, and then Bella picked up her menu. She couldn't remember the last time she'd had good sushi. Deciding was going to be hard.

In the end she got miso soup to start and twelve assorted sushi rolls, choosing to stay simple with her choices. "I won't be able to eat all twelve," she said. "We can share."

He nodded. "Why don't I make a few choices and we can just share everything?"

That sounded perfect, so when the server came back Bella ordered her soup and the rolls, while Burke added his own soup, as well as edamame and sashimi. Bella's stomach growled in anticipation and Burke chuckled. "Looks like we got here just in time."

"I've been too nervous to eat much."

"You were really worried, huh?"

She nodded. "I can't thank you enough, Burke. For what you did for us in Italy and for getting

Maman in to see Dr. Mallick so quickly. She'll be on the road to recovery much faster now."

"I was happy to. And blockages are nothing to play with. She's been having these attacks for a while. I don't think she wanted you to know how long."

Bella frowned. "Why would she wait to see a doctor?"

He shrugged. "Fear? Or just telling herself it was stress or whatever."

"Then I'm doubly glad you were there to bully her into going."

He lifted an eyebrow. "I don't think anyone bullies Aurora Pemberton into anything."

"You're right," she conceded. "Must be your charm."

He opened his mouth to respond but just then the server came back with their appetizers. The miso smelled heavenly, and Bella dipped her spoon in for a taste while Burke went for the edamame first.

They made more casual conversation as they ate, first the soup, and then the sushi that arrived looking fresh and colorful and scrumptious. The wasabi was delightfully hot and the spicy tuna roll was perfection. She reached for another roll with her chopsticks and clashed with Burke's.

"En garde," he joked.

"I'll fight you for the salmon avocado roll," she replied, jabbing his chopsticks with hers.

He laughed. "Maybe we can negotiate for it."

Her eyes narrowed. "Hmm. Depends on what you're offering."

His gaze settled on hers and he said, simply, "You can have it if you stay with me tonight, instead of at the hotel."

She nearly dropped her chopsticks. It was a most unexpected proposition, and one she knew she must turn down. She knew what he was asking. It wasn't a "stay at my place because it's convenient" thing. They were past that sort of platonic invitation, even though in truth they'd only shared a single, fairly chaste kiss. He wasn't offering his spare bed. He was asking her to stay…with him. Charlotte's earlier words rang in her ears. Did she really want to miss out on this kind of opportunity, with a man like him?

And yet…how well did she really know him? She knew he was kind, and that he liked helping people, and that he didn't seem to care a jot that he held any sort of title. But there was so much more beneath the surface.

How would he feel if he knew that she had never been with a man before? He'd retract his invitation, and that would be humiliating to the extreme. And yet how could she explain to him why she was saying no? He deserved for her to be honest but even being honest made her so very vulnerable. She was doomed either way.

"You can have it," she said, withdrawing her chopsticks.

He didn't move, just held her gaze evenly as his lips formed a pout. "At least tell me you're tempted. My pride deserves that much."

Why did he always manage to make her want to laugh? "I'm tempted, okay? But Burke...that's... I mean..." She let out a breath and tried to gather her thoughts. "I'm not good at being casual with this sort of thing." She waited for lightning to strike her on the spot. Being casual? Being anything! She figured she was blushing and hoped it wasn't noticeable. Thirty years old and still a virgin. She figured that must be some sort of record, and not one she was going to advertise.

"Did I say anything about being casual?" He leaned closer. "What if I told you that I'm not ready for the day to end? I want to spend it with you. To have the chance to really get to know you." He reached for her hand, still holding the chopsticks. "The way I should have all those years ago, when I was too busy being an idiot."

She bit down on her lip. He had seen the marks on her skin and didn't seem to care, did he? And yes, he'd been an idiot, but she could easily pin some of that blame on her brothers. "Listen, Stephen and William made you promise. And I decided to show you what you were missing. There is enough blame about that night to go around."

"It is what it is," he agreed. "But it doesn't have

to stay that way. I want to spend today with you. I want to spend the night with you. Be with you in the morning and take you to the hospital to get your mum. To sit with you when you drink your morning tea."

Is this what being wooed was like? She liked it. And he remembered that she drank tea, not coffee, in the mornings.

Still, it seemed too soon to make any promises. She needed time to think if this was really what she wanted. If she was ready. Odd question, considering her age. And if she were going to trust anyone, it would be Burke. She'd forgiven the boy he'd been that first night at the Baresi villa. Since then he'd done nothing to make her think she couldn't trust him.

"Can I think about it?" she asked, and butterflies went winging through her belly as soon as she said it, opening the door to the possibility.

"Of course you can. Just remember that I care about you. I'm crazy attracted to you. That's not going to change if you say no."

At the moment she was thinking he was rather too good to be true. He had to have a flaw somewhere, but she'd yet to find it. And that made her uncomfortable.

"You have the salmon roll anyway," he said, sitting back and smiling. "I'm getting full."

He'd eaten most of the sashimi, and there were only a few rolls left. Bella swiped some wasabi onto the salmon roll and popped it in her mouth, savoring the spicy heat. When it was gone, they were too full for any sort of dessert. Burke paid the bill, and they made the walk back to the hospital.

"Aurora should be awake now," he said. "And definitely more alert. Do you want to go see her?"

"Very much." She wanted to see for herself that her mother was all right. To make sure she wasn't having any pain. Burke would be there, too, and would know what to look for.

They went back in the hospital, making their way to Aurora's room. Burke's invitation still rang in Bella's ears. Could she do it? Was Burke the man she would finally sleep with?

She had to stop thinking so much, or the significance of it was going to grow to gigantic proportions. He cared about her, but he was still only offering one night, not a marriage proposal. She needed to remember that. The most important thing was that no matter what she chose, he must never know she was a virgin. For both their sakes.

# CHAPTER SEVEN

AURORA WAS SITTING up in bed, still wearing the hospital gown, but looking none the worse for wear. Bella had stopped and picked up a bottle of orange juice and a small sandwich in case Aurora hadn't eaten yet. She'd fasted before the procedure, and now it was midafternoon.

"Maman," Bella said, happy to see healthy color in her mother's cheeks. "You did great. Dr. Mallick said you did brilliantly."

"I'm supposed to go slowly for a while, and I might be crazy, but I think I already feel better."

Burke smiled and leaned over and kissed her cheek. "The stent keeps the artery open. The increased blood flow makes a big difference in how you feel. Are you hungry? Bella picked up a snack for you."

"I wasn't for a while. The sedative made me a bit nauseated. But I might be able to eat."

"It's just juice and a sandwich. But I can get you something else—"

"Nonsense, darling, this is fine." For all Aurora's wealth and status, deep down she was not a diva. Bella had always liked that about her. When they'd been kids, they'd never been allowed to throw tantrums about not liking a gift or wanting something better. They'd had to at least try everything that was put on the table. Bella had always credited it to her mother's very humble beginnings. She'd married into her wealth; she hadn't been born into it.

Bella uncapped the juice and poured it into a cup. "Here. It's cold."

Aurora took a long drink and let out a happy sigh. "That's lovely. Just missing champagne."

Burke and Bella laughed. "No mimosas for you for a day or two," Burke warned.

"Did you two eat? You've been here all day." She looked up from her juice, her gaze shifting between them.

"Burke took me for sushi nearby, once we'd spoken to your doctor. We thought it would give you time to wake up."

"Good."

"Is there anything we can get you, Maman? The evening is bound to be a long one." Bella almost wished there'd be something. It would give her an excuse…a way to not have to make a decision about going to Burke's.

"No, thank you, Bella. I actually brought a book and some magazines. I'm going to take the opportunity to just rest. With work and the commotion with the wedding, a night to not do anything sounds like a treat." She cast a sideways glance at Burke. "Even if I do have to wear this awful gown."

"You can change out of it if you like," he said. "If you brought something comfortable."

"I can help you," Bella offered.

"Bella, I can dress myself. You don't need to hover."

Bella sat on the bed and looked into Aurora's face. "Indulge me. I've been horribly worried about you."

"I know." Aurora softened her voice. "And I'm so thankful you've been with me the past few days. You've been a real calm support, which is just what I needed. But today? I'm just going to read some magazines and get some extra rest. Tomorrow, when we go home, you can fuss all you want."

"Promise?"

Aurora chuckled. "I'll regret this, but I promise. Please, go enjoy an evening out. When was the last time you really had one? And don't say Italy. William's wedding doesn't count."

So much for having an excuse.

"Only if you're sure. And if you want anything at all, I have my mobile. I'll be back in the morning and then we'll get you out of here and back to the manor. Mrs. Flanagan and the cook are ready to spoil you rotten with healthy meals. I hear they've been scouring books and websites to find heart-healthy recipes with your favorite foods."

Burke looked over at Bella. "Mrs. Flanagan is still with you?"

She nodded. "You remember her?"

"I do. Red hair, right? Daughter about our age, maybe a bit younger?"

Bella nodded. "You've got a good memory."

"You two should catch up," Aurora said. "Go on. I'm going to eat my sandwich and then maybe nap again. I won't have this much solitude for a while."

Bella kissed her mother on her head and Burke gave Aurora's hand a squeeze. "Any pain, anything that doesn't feel right, you hit that call bell for the nurse, all right? They already have instructions to call Dr. Mallick and me."

"Thank you, dear. I will. I promise."

They left her room and Bella started to giggle. "Oh, my. My mother just called you 'dear.' You're about to bump Stephen from the Golden Boy pedestal."

Burke laughed. "I doubt it. But if being here gave your mother peace of mind, I was happy to do it."

She hesitated when they got to the elevator. "Burke, about your offer…"

He looked over at her, and his eyes took on an intensity that both frightened and exhilarated her.

The thing was, she wanted to. And after all this time, she was starting to think it would be better to get it over with. Her virginity was becoming an albatross she couldn't shake.

But she'd told him that she couldn't be casual, and that was the deep-down truth. She wanted him. The kiss on the plane had been a mere taster. What if it had been just the surprise of it that had caused such a reaction? What if this was all blown out of proportion? On impulse, she took a step toward him and pressed her mouth to his.

After a flicker of surprise, he relaxed and kissed her back, his lips warm and tempting. A delicious shiver ran over her body as his tongue slipped into her mouth. She nearly lifted her hand to slide into his hair when the elevator chimed and the doors started to open.

She jumped back as if the contact burned her, and moved to make space for the people getting on the elevator.

But the truth was his kiss was hot fire and not just "pleasant." The heat of it raced through her veins, making her want things she usually could resist. And yet she didn't want to promise something she couldn't necessarily follow through on. If she said yes, and then froze…she'd feel like an idiot. The humiliation would be awful.

They reached the ground floor and the doors opened. The other passengers got out first, then

Bella, with Burke's wide hand resting lightly on the hollow of her back. "Bella?" he asked.

She turned and faced him, aware they were in a busy public area, but knowing this was the moment she had to decide. She looked into his face and took a deep breath. "Here's the thing," she said, trying to keep her voice down. "If I say yes to spending the night, I still want… I need… oh, damn. I need to know that it doesn't have to mean sex if…" Heat rushed to her face and neck and she slid her gaze away from him.

But he put his hand under her chin and cupped it gently, turning it so that she faced him again. "You always, always have the right to say no. I want you, Bella. I'll be honest about that. I want you to stay with me tonight. But if we get there and you decide you need to sleep in the spare room…then that's where you'll sleep."

"And you…"

He gave her a sideways smile. "I can take care of myself."

She caught the double meaning in his words and tried not to laugh. He made her feel so beautiful, so desirable. No man had ever done that for her before. Honestly, she tended to deliberately put herself in the background. Charlotte had been the Pemberton sister to get all the attention. It felt nice to be wooed, if she was being truthful with herself.

And she wanted to spend more time with

him. After tomorrow she'd be going back to Chatsworth Manor until the beginning of the week, and then to Paris next week to work in the office full-time. Her mother was taking an entire month off, which meant that Bella would be in charge for a minimum of three weeks. She wasn't sure she was ready. Tonight could be her last hurrah for a while. Why not spend it with someone whose company she truly enjoyed? And who seemed to enjoy hers, not out of professional obligation but just because?

"What did you have in mind?" she asked. It was still afternoon. The idea that he'd been thinking they'd rush off to his place and fall in bed for the rest of the day made her incredibly anxious. If she were going to be with him she had to work up to it gradually.

He checked his watch and frowned. "It's just after three. But I have an idea. Something I think you'd really enjoy." He took her hand. "Come on."

He pulled her forward, and once they were outside in the summer heat again, he hailed a taxi. She half heard him give instructions to the driver as she climbed in, and then he made a quick phone call as they sped away, leaving the hospital and her mother behind.

"Where are we going?"

He tucked his phone back in his pants pocket and grinned. "It's a surprise. One of my favorite places in London, actually. And we should be there in maybe ten minutes."

She was intrigued and sat back in her seat, determined to enjoy the spontaneity. There'd been so little of that in her adult life that it was a strange but not unwelcome sensation. There'd been no "whisking away" on mystery dates. No propositions over sushi. This was turning out to be a day of many firsts, it seemed.

The taxi zipped into South London and it seemed like in no time at all that they were at the Horniman Museum. She tilted her head a bit, wondering what about this made it his favorite place in the city. He paid the driver, they popped out, and he took her hand. "Ready?"

The Horniman Museum and Gardens covered over sixteen acres, featuring a number of gardens, a meadow, the main museum, and various other buildings. They entered at the north end, and Burke took her hand again and headed straight to the entrance of the butterfly house.

Butterflies. Her fascination intensified.

There was a family waiting to gain entrance, and Burke looked at his watch. "We made it. Last entrance is at three thirty. This family will go in and then we've got the last slot of the day."

She squinted as she looked up at him. "You are full of surprises."

"I'm glad to hear it." He smiled down at her.

"It's going to be warm in there. You might be a bit toasty."

She'd chosen bone-colored linen trousers and sandals for the day; cool enough, she supposed, and certainly cooler than Burke's khakis. But while he wore short sleeves, she had on a peasant top in sage green, the sleeves dropping to past her elbows, and her hair was pulled back in a partial braid from the sides, before trailing halfway down her back.

"I'll be fine." She smiled faintly. Making accommodations due to her injuries had become such a long-standing habit that it surprised her to realize she felt a bit resentful of it in this moment. What would she give to simply coil her hair up in a messy topknot and let the air at her nape? Small things to anyone else. And yet the thought of it made her stomach twist just a bit.

The family entered and then they advanced in line. "Burke Phillips," he stated.

"Oh, Mr. Phillips, hello." The young girl working admission looked to be a summer student, perhaps, and her cheeks pinkened at the sight of Burke. Why not, after all? He was ridiculously handsome. "You're our last entrance of the day. It'll just be a few minutes."

"Thanks," he replied, and they waited silently.

It wasn't long and she checked her watch. "Oh, you might as well go ahead. It's only five minutes. Just a reminder that we close in half an hour."

"Perfect. Thank you so much."

They entered and Bella looked behind her at the girl, then at Burke. "She didn't charge you!" Her mouth had dropped open. "Did you just get in here for free because you batted your handsome eyelashes?"

He laughed. "No, I got in for free because I'm a benefactor. I told you, it's one of my favorite places. I make a donation every year."

Well, that was a relief. "Oh."

"I love that your mind went that way, though." He chuckled again. "Jealous, darling?"

She didn't want to answer that. Instead she asked the obvious question as they moved into the house and the heat and humidity hit. "So why is this on your list?"

Burke's feet stopped and he faced her. "I spent a lot of weekend mornings here. My mother used to bring us several times a year. We'd visit the butterfly house, the museum, the aquarium, walk the gardens. Then we'd go to the café and she'd let us order whatever we liked, no matter what time of day it was. Those are good childhood memories."

And he was sharing it with her. He was so open. So comfortable with himself, and that was something she couldn't relate to at all. She was really beginning to understand how high and thick the walls were that she'd built around herself. They were invisible and innocuous until someone like Burke came along and made her realize how big they really were. Did she even know who the real Bella was? Or was she someone constructed after one dreadful, life-altering mistake?

"Are you all right?" He was peering down at her with concern. "You look upset. Should I not have brought you here?"

She shook her head quickly. "No, this is lovely. I'm just…in awe of you. You share so easily. I don't know how to do that."

"It takes a while to learn," he admitted. "I was pretty withdrawn for a while. Honestly, your brother helped me a lot. He knew what had happened, and when we met again at university, his friendship…it meant a lot. He was the one guy who knew my secret and liked me anyway. But before then… I didn't share at all."

"I haven't, either. Only surface stuff," she admitted.

"Don't worry, Bella. I still have a few secrets."

They walked along slowly. Bella found her breath slowing as she relaxed, despite the moist heat. The quiet, the tropical plants, the soft flitting of butterflies…it all soothed. She smiled as a butterfly landed on Burke's shoulder, the colors striking with black and white spots and a stunning shade of orange in toward the body. "Don't move," she said, and she reached for her phone to take a picture.

To her surprise, the butterfly stayed perched there, so light and fragile, and she snapped the photo. "It's so gorgeous. I wish I knew what kind it was."

"A leopard lacewing," he stated softly.

Of course he would know.

"What do we do now?"

"Leave it be and carry on. It'll move on when it's ready."

Her smile grew. This was such a lovely way to spend the afternoon, even if she was sweating from the humidity. She lifted her hair and fanned her neck a bit, and Burke looked over, his eyes wide with what she now considered his "soulful" look, one that must inspire so much trust in his patients. "What?"

"You should just put it up if it bothers you. We're the last ones in here. No one will see."

He was right. They were alone and she was sweltering in the heat between the pants, the long sleeves, and the weight of her hair. "Give me a moment," she said, and then with quick fingers she slid the elastic out of her braid, shook out the plait, and then gathered up the whole mass and twisted it up into a coil. She used the elastic to anchor it, though the band didn't feel quite up to the task. "It won't hold forever, but it does feel better."

"I'm glad."

And if anything more happened tonight, he'd see her scars again. The one on the back of her neck was probably her angriest one, though.

They meandered through the butterfly house. In some spots, plates were set out with sweet fruit, and clusters of butterflies could be found congregating, eating their fill. There were plaques throughout explaining life stages and signage marking the tropical foliage, but she most enjoyed it when Burke pointed out the ones he knew: the large owl butterflies, gray and brown, with large spots that looked like owl eyes on their wings; stunning black-and-green emerald butterflies, the vibrant green matching the leaves on which they sat. Dozens of them flitted through the air, and one settled on the top of Bella's topknot. Burke used her phone to take a picture and told her she should call it "hair accessories." That led her to talking about Charlotte and Jacob, and how he'd given her a butterfly pendant to show how she'd grown and changed.

"Charlotte was so good at what she did. And she was Aurora Inc. from top to toe. Always wore black and white, the signature colors. But she was hiding herself behind what she thought were expectations. Since she met Jacob, she's really blossomed into someone even more spectacular."

"We're all hiding behind something. Expectations is a good one."

"What are you hiding behind, Burke?"

"Guilt."

She stopped as the light tone of the conversation turned to something weightier. "I'm sorry. That's a tough one. Self-forgiveness… I don't know. It's easier to forgive someone else than yourself."

"Nailed it," he answered. "And what do you hide behind, Bella?"

She thought for a moment. She didn't hide behind her scars—she hid because of them. "Fear," she finally said, her throat tight.

"Of what?"

Another butterfly perched on her finger. She could barely breathe; she didn't want to disturb the beautiful creatures who felt safe enough to alight on her body. "Of people knowing I'm not perfect. My family isn't perfect but outwardly? We don't show our flaws. I don't want to be…" She hesitated.

"The only one?"

"Yes," she breathed. "I don't want to be the only one, the focus of curiosity and pity and speculation. I have never wanted that kind of attention, not even in positive ways."

"But in doing that, you haven't let you be you, either," he reasoned. "Bella."

She looked up, shocked to see tears in his eyes.

He swallowed, his throat bobbing with the effort. "If I had stopped Royce that night, if I hadn't listened to your brothers, you would have been spared all this. He'd still be alive. I failed everyone that night, and I'm so sorry. You're stuck in this prison you've made around yourself all because I was a jackass."

She ignored the butterfly on her hand and reached out to him. The butterfly flew off with a delicate flap of its wings. "It was not your fault! I was so determined to show you what you were missing I went along with Royce even though I knew it was stupid! You came along...why did you do that?"

"Because I wanted to make sure you were all right. Instead, when everything happened, I couldn't even help you."

The truth of that settled around her as she put herself in his shoes. He'd gone along to keep an eye on her, and instead he'd ended up unconscious and unable to assist at all. For someone like him—who was driven to help people—that must have been a tough pill to swallow.

She bit down on her lip. "We can't change what happened. And if I've built a prison around myself, well, that's on me. My decision to make. When I was younger my family tried to tell me I was isolating myself too much. I buried myself in the cosmetics side of the business, trying new things, learning new techniques, all so I could better hide. That is not on you, Burke. And if you spend your entire life trying to redeem yourself because of one mistake, you're going to end up dissatisfied. Like me. Let go. If it's forgiveness you need, you have it. Though there's nothing to forgive."

It was the most she'd ever said to anyone about the emotions associated with her scars. It was understood to be a nonstarter for discussion in the Pemberton household. But it felt good to say it all now. And the fact that she trusted Burke with it was both astounding and frightening.

She stepped away from him, moving to the next curve in the path through the display, needing the space. She turned around and faced him, but he didn't move. He just waited, staring at her, while everything they'd just admitted settled around them, the weight of it fragile and even beautiful.

She lifted her arms a little and realized half a dozen little butterflies had gravitated to her blouse. They were everywhere, and she caught her breath as one perched precariously on the tip of her nose. She looked past it to Burke, who was smiling widely, his phone out, snapping pictures. And then she couldn't help it either. She smiled back, a wondrous feeling made up of so many emotions she couldn't list them all. It was just a beautiful, expansive feeling that was somehow calming and grounding and perfect.

He came to her then, but didn't touch her. "They're too fragile," he said softly. "I don't want to damage one. We'll keep going and staff will inspect us for any random travelers before we leave."

"We're okay?" she asked, needing to be sure. They'd covered some heavy ground.

"We're more than okay," he replied. "What you said… I'm still not sure I believe you. But it means more than you know." His gaze delved into hers, so intense she was afraid she might lose herself in it. "I wish I could kiss you right now. But the lacewing on your nose has moved to your hairline and I'm afraid of smushing it."

"You can kiss me later," she replied, surprising herself with her boldness.

"I'm counting on it."

When they reached the exit, one of the staff had to remove the hangers-on. There was no time for Bella to put her hair down, but to her relief the young man assisting her never even blinked at the sight of the ugly white line across her neck. He just did his job, smiling and chatting the whole time, and then she was outside again with Burke, where the air was still summery but not nearly as humid and hot.

"Let's take a walk in the gardens," he suggested, and held out his hand.

She left her hair in the floppy knot and twined her fingers with his.

# CHAPTER EIGHT

BURKE HELD HER hand as they walked through the gardens in the waning afternoon. The entrances wouldn't close for hours, and they had the luxury of meandering to enjoy the fresh, fragranced air.

What she'd said inside, about forgiveness—both about how hard it was to forgive himself, and also offering hers—he'd had to hold himself together and it had been tough. He'd tried to do the right thing that night all around and had failed miserably at it all. He hadn't responded to her flirting because of her brothers. But he'd watched over her just the same, and made the wrong decision to keep her safe. To keep all of them safe. Royce had died. Fiona had sustained minor injuries, but a person didn't walk away from that sort of accident without lingering emotions. And Bella...she'd paid a high price as well. She was marked for life.

But she didn't blame him. She took responsibility for her own actions. Did she know how strong she was? How rare? Who was he to judge her for wanting to keep her scars hidden in an industry that demanded perfection? Who was he to judge at all when he carried his own secrets around, hidden away from the world? All this talk about forgiveness…and he still hadn't found a way to forgive his father. And now his dad was gone and forgiveness was moot anyway. Still, what kind of a man was he who wanted to be forgiven but couldn't find it within himself to do the same?

She'd left her hair up this afternoon. He glanced over and saw the jagged lines just below her hairline. Other than in the pool, he had never seen her with her hair up. In the butterfly house they'd been alone. Now there were lots of other people milling about.

He got the feeling this was a big step for her.

They wandered past the prehistoric garden, their pace slow and lazy. Conversation, too, was light, which he appreciated as he absorbed what had happened inside. They read about different plants and environments, remarking on items of interest. The sunken garden was glorious, a riot of color but all set so precisely in the center. Bella surprised him by taking a selfie of them together. She seemed so…free. It was a marked change from the woman he'd been drawn to in Italy and the worried daughter from this morning. He liked the change. A lot.

They carried on to the bandstand, which he

knew had the most amazing view of the city. Bella stopped and took a deep breath when they reached the top of the hill. "Oh. This is stunning! I wish I had a different camera. My phone just doesn't quite cut it."

The city lay below them, peaks and spires and high rises, with the Shard dominating them all. A haze had settled over the buildings there, creating a dreamlike quality.

"Good choice for the afternoon?" he asked.

"The best!" She turned to him, her smile wide. "I didn't realize how much I needed something like this. It's been wedding and work and worry about Maman for days. Thank you, Burke. This has been perfect. Even the weather has cooperated."

"No summer showers...yet," he added.

"It could rain for all I care." She reached out and put her hand on his arm. "You've made what might have been a very stressful day into something I'll remember for a long time."

He wanted to say that there could be many more afternoons like this, but could there be, really? He'd asked her to spend the night with him. He wanted that. Wanted her. But was it fair? His work was here, and yes, Chatsworth was not that long a drive, but it wasn't her permanent home. That was Paris.

Maybe he should withdraw his invitation, but how would she take that? As a rejection? It certainly wasn't. And it seemed presumptive to have a "relationship" talk at this early stage. It wasn't casual, but it wasn't not casual. It was…complicated.

"What's wrong?" she asked.

"Nothing." He smiled at her again. "Absolutely nothing."

"Good. Because I think you need to stop thinking and just enjoy the day." Her smile was wide, her eyes bright.

It was good advice, and he decided to take it. They could just let things play out organically tonight, couldn't they?

After their long walk, they were both hungry. It was Bella who suggested dinner. "Let's eat at my hotel," she said. "The restaurant there is amazing and I'd like to treat you, Burke. You've done so much for me, and for Maman."

The hotel. She'd said she was going to stay with him, but the hotel gave her a reason to go either way. Either she'd grab her bag and leave with him, or he'd leave after dinner—alone. Still, he couldn't refuse her. He rather suspected he couldn't refuse her anything if she asked, and that was a bit worrying.

They took a cab back to her hotel in Westminster. They hadn't made reservations, but a word from Bella and they were escorted to a table by the window. She'd taken her hair out of the elastic in the cab, and had run her fingers through it, creating a waterfall of dark waves that he longed to sink his hands into. They were dressed a bit casually for the setting, but that didn't affect their service at all. Within moments they were given menus and Bella ordered them a bottle of fine red.

When they were alone again, Bella asked, "Do you mind if I text Maman to check in with her?"

"Of course not. Why would I?"

She laughed. "We have a family rule about tech at the table. Started when we got our first phones and it's stuck."

"I give you permission." He grinned at her. "You know, sometimes the Pembertons really seem like a normal family."

She lifted a shoulder in a shrug. "You mean, other than the money, the properties, the titles, the servants?"

"That's exactly what I mean." He grinned as she tapped in a quick message. "It's one of the reasons I liked William so much. Everyone did, actually."

"He's a lovable guy."

"It runs in the family." He was gratified when she blushed yet again. He was trying to be subtle with his flirting, easing their way into the rest of the evening, no matter what choice she made.

"I think I'm going to start with the baked camembert and then have the quail," she said, putting her menu aside. "Newsflash: I love cheese."

He scanned the menu. "And I think I'll have the duck croquette and then the sea bass." He also put his menu aside. "I haven't been here in ages. Even if it is close to work."

"No bringing your hot dates out for some fine French cuisine?"

"I don't really date. To be honest, I don't want to date anyone where I work, because that can get messy. And I work a lot, so…"

She lifted an eyebrow. Their wine arrived and once it was poured he watched Bella take a long sip. "Oh, that's lovely," she said, closing her eyes. How had he not noticed how sensual she was before?

The wine was delicious, and so was their food, though to Burke's surprise he was so wrapped up in talking that he was surprised when his plate was empty and they were offered dessert.

Bella looked up at the server and smiled. "Opera cake, *s'il vous plaît*."

He loved that she didn't refuse dessert but instead went for something rich and decadent. "I'll have the *tarte tatin*," he said. And when the server was gone, he poured the rest of the wine from the bottle into their glasses.

"This was really nice," Bella said, sitting back in her chair. She looked utterly relaxed, for the first time since he'd seen her in the Baresi kitchen. Did that mean she was comfortable with him? He let his gaze cling to hers as he lifted his glass, slowly sipping the rich wine. They'd spent the entire day together, and it wasn't over yet. At least he hoped.

"You have bedroom eyes," she said, toying with her glass. "When you look at me that way."

There were things he might have said had they not been in a public restaurant, so instead he let a smile tease the corners of his lips. "Only when I look at you, Bella."

Appreciation lighted her eyes. "And you're a smooth talker."

"I only tell the truth."

"That's a very dangerous statement to make. It really locks you in, you know."

"Ask me anything." His breath held after he said it.

"Your favorite color."

"Green."

"Guilty pleasure for food."

Easy. "Fish and chips. In paper, with lots of vinegar."

"Mmm…yummy. Theme song?"

He considered his glass. "Hmm, that's a tough one. Pass, while I think about it."

"Thing you're most proud of."

Another easy one. "Graduating from medical school."

"The one thing you'd never want people to know about you."

He halted, brought up short by that question.

The lightning round quality to the first questions had been light and somewhat predictable. This, though…he lifted his glass and drained what was left in it. He thought of his father and the wine burned down his throat and into his stomach. But that…he didn't own his father's guilt. He reminded himself of that often. "The accident," he said hoarsely. "So maybe we're more alike than you thought after all. I don't want people to look at me differently because of what happened. As they surely would. I've worked so hard at building my reputation. Of trying to outlive what happened. But it feels very much like a house of cards that could come tumbling down. So you see, Bella, I can't criticize you for hiding your scars. Because I'm hiding mine, too."

As quiet fell between them, their desserts came. It gave Burke time to reset the mood, take it from something so heavy to something more fun and intimate. "Okay. Enough about me. Your turn. Favorite color."

"Blue."

"Guilty pleasure in the food department."

"Chocolate. And ice cream."

He filed that one away for future reference. He decided against the theme song and instead asked, "What do you consider the perfect date?"

Her smile blossomed. "Today."

Now he was getting somewhere.

"The one thing you wish people knew about you."

Her eyes darkened, just a little, as her gaze met his and held. "I'm not always as practical as I seem."

"Ah." He nodded, his body tensing in a delicious way. "Hidden passions."

"You could say that."

"Arabella Pemberton, always in control."

"Appearances can be misleading."

He had a premonition of her being out of control and had to take a long, slow breath. "I think we should eat our dessert," he said roughly.

Her eyes held a spark of challenge. "Chicken," she said, and then her smile lifted on one side, mocking him, and he realized he loved her subtle but sharp sense of humor.

He hoped beyond hope that she was leaving the hotel with him tonight.

Bella had already made her choice, but their conversation over dinner had sealed it. She dipped her fork into the luscious cake and fought back the nerves about what was to come. Today Burke had been very open with her, sharing his own insecurities. It was clear that the physical attraction was a real thing and she liked him…a lot. Moreover, she trusted him as much as she'd ever trusted anyone. Today had been the perfect date. She hadn't lied about that. The butterfly house and the gardens and a romantic dinner…there wasn't a single part of it that hadn't been absolutely lovely.

"Your cake looks amazing."

"Here, try some." She put some on her fork and held it out, and he leaned forward and closed his lips around it. She was mesmerized by the sight of them touching the tines, taking the cake into his mouth. She wanted to kiss him again, badly. To be held in his arms and to have the time to kiss him properly, without sneaking it in an airplane galley or a briefly empty elevator.

"Mmm…delicious."

"It is. And rich. But every now and then you have to treat yourself."

The rest of dessert seemed to take too long. When they were finally finished, and Bella signaled for the bill, a slight awkwardness fell over them. Burke was waiting, she knew. Waiting for her to confirm what she'd said earlier. She'd chosen the hotel restaurant deliberately, because if she got cold feet it would be easy to go upstairs and spend the evening alone, as planned. But she wasn't going to do that. She was going to grab her overnight bag, drop her key and go with him. To his place.

Burke reached over and took her hand when she signed the slip to charge the meal to the room. "Bella," he said, his voice hesitant.

"Let me go upstairs and get my things," she

replied quietly. "I'll drop my key in the express checkout for the morning."

His eyes widened.

"I wasn't sure, either," she said. "But I am now."

They got up from the table and she put a hand on his arm. "Wait for me in the lobby. I'll be back soon."

She took the elevator upstairs, her heart pounding the whole time. She was mostly sure of what she was doing, and the little bit that wasn't sure, she understood was nerves because this was a Big Deal. Inside the room, she took a few minutes to tuck her things into her small bag and clear her toiletries out of the bathroom. Her throat tightened as she thought of the hours ahead. Would it be wonderful? Awkward? Disappointing? Her hand paused on the door handle. Burke. Of all the men over the years, she'd chosen Burke. He was the only one who knew what happened to her, who had seen how badly she'd been marked, and he wanted her anyway.

It was time to go.

She closed the hotel room door behind her and made her way down in the elevator again. Burke hadn't moved from his spot in the lobby, and she took a hidden moment to study him. He was such a gentleman. And sexy and smart and... there wasn't much to not like about him, really. Eventually she knew she'd have to discover his flaws, but right now she was enjoying him being rather perfect.

He turned when she approached, a smile lighting his face, warming her from the inside out. "Ready?" he asked.

At Burke's suggestion, they took the tube to Piccadilly Circus and then switched and got off at Green Park. It was his usual route to work, he said, unless he needed the fresh air and brisk walk. His flat was only a five-minute walk from the station, and he solicitously carried Bella's bag over his shoulder as they entered his building.

"When did you move out of the family home?" she asked as they climbed the stairs to his flat.

"When I got the job at the hospital. I was hardly ever there anyway, what with being away at school. It hadn't really been home for some time."

"I feel the same," she admitted. "We have the manor house and the château in Provence. But those are places to visit. We all have our own flats or houses."

"And yours is in Paris."

"It is. Stephen has one there, and William, too. Charlotte has moved out of hers and is living with Jacob in Richmond. Though if she comes over, she stays with either Maman or me. It's been nice, having sisterly sleepovers."

He opened his door and let her in first.

The space was very Burke. Welcoming and

comfortable, but also modern and somehow light. His furniture was simple, a gray sofa and chair with a glass-topped coffee table on a printed rug. To the left Bella saw the kitchen and caught a glimpse of the brushed steel finish on the appliances and fixtures. "I like it," she said, turning around and smiling at him. "It's like walking into an Ikea showroom."

He laughed. "Would it be wrong to say 'busted'? There might just be a few items from that store in this flat." He took her bag. "Let me show you the rest."

The rest consisted of a lovely bathroom with a claw-foot tub and hexagonal shower, a bedroom decorated in blues and pale yellows, looking fresh and appealing, and then his bedroom, which went back to the gray color scheme again, with dove-gray on the walls and a gray-and-black duvet on the king-sized bed. The bed took up half the room, while a dresser and nightstand rounded out the furniture.

"Again, very you," she said, trying to keep her voice light. But ever since they'd entered his room, that awkward pall had fallen over them again. She knew it was just nerves. What surprised her was that they seemed to be coming from him as well as her.

One of them being nervous was bad enough.

He put her bag down by the dresser, then met her eyes. Let out a breath. When the silence drew out for three or four seconds, he asked, "Would you like a drink?"

She would. Desperately. Her nerves were coiled tighter than a spring.

He led her out of the bedroom, but grasped her hand in his and kept it there, forming a connection that felt sweet but also very intentional. In the kitchen, he took a bottle of cabernet off the counter and reached for two glasses in a cabinet.

"You seem to prefer red."

"I do." She took the glass from his fingers and added, "It's supposed to be good for your heart."

A slow smile graced his lips as his eyes warmed to dark, chocolaty pools. She could lose herself in them, she realized, and with that came the knowledge that she wanted to. And yet… she was horribly afraid that she'd do something wrong, something silly that would give away her inexperience. She had no idea what to do right now. Anything that happened would be the beginning of something, and she was walking into totally new territory.

She would not think about how she was going through this at thirty when most women had conquered this mountain in their teens, or at least early twenties.

Instead she drank the wine, holding his gaze, wanting him to make the first move so she didn't have to. He took a drink as well, then put his glass on the counter to her right before moving closer. So close that his body was almost touching hers, and she could easily reach out and touch him.

Her glass shook in her hand.

He took it from her and placed it beside his, then turned his attention back to her, his smile gone. His clear, knowing eyes, the set of his mouth…so serious. As if he somehow understood the gravity of this moment though he couldn't possibly.

He put his hand along her face, just like he had in Italy, and then leaned forward to kiss her. It was soft and slow, giving her time to be sure, to respond and to give back rather than just take. She did, kissing him, sliding her hands around his ribs to rest on his back as his lips and tongue did delicious things, stoking her desire.

She did desire him. The need rising up in her was new and demanding, but she promised herself she wouldn't let her body get ahead of her head or her heart. So she let the sensation wash over her, taking her time. He was, after all, an excellent kisser, and there was no need to rush past this delightful introduction.

Burke nudged against her and her hips bumped the countertop, so that she was braced between it and his hard, strong body. She let her hands run on instinct and they pulled his shirt out of his pants and then slid beneath the fabric to the warm skin beneath. He caught his breath—were her hands cold? His skin was smooth and warm, and she wanted to feel herself pressed against it.

But to do that she'd have to remove her top, and she wasn't ready for that stage yet. Just the thought cooled her actions a little, and she paused the motion of her fingers.

"Don't stop," he murmured against her lips. "Your hands feel so good."

"You feel good," she said in reply, the sound muffled against his cheek as his lips slid from hers and skated along her jawline, creating shivers down her arms. Her whole body was now on full alert.

"You taste good," he added, and he pulled her earlobe into his mouth. A strangled sound passed her lips, and she was mortified, until he started kissing her again, with more urgency. So he'd liked it…

He slid his hand under her loose top and rested his palm on the curve of her waist. Nothing serious, nothing pushy…and yet her body strained forward, urging him to cup her breast. They were aching for his touch now, and when he didn't move his hand, she reached down and did it for him, sliding it up until it covered her breast and the hard tip pressed into his palm.

These sensations were not entirely foreign. She'd been seventeen when the accident had happened, after all, and had dated and fooled around as any teenager would. Even since then, she'd dated some, kissed, enjoyed some harmless touching. But she'd always stopped short, right around this point, unwilling to go any further and make herself vulnerable. This was the moment, then, where she either moved forward or halted what was happening between them.

Stopping was the last thing she wanted to do, both in her body and in her mind, and despite the fears and insecurities battling inside her.

His thumb flicked over her nipple and she inhaled sharply, felt herself tremble. Burke leaned close and murmured in her ear, "I'll take care of you, Bella."

He couldn't know. There was no way. Her sister didn't even know. But he'd said exactly the right thing because she knew he was the one she could trust. He'd already seen and hadn't run away. Not even close.

She reached for the buttons on his shirt and started undoing them, ignoring how badly her fingers were shaking. She pushed the shirt off his shoulders and admired his flat abs and broad chest. She'd gotten a good look at his upper body in the pool at the Baresi villa but now she could touch it and she did so, finding it smooth and warm. His eyes fluttered shut at her light touch and she marveled that she had the power to evoke that kind of a response. When his lids lifted, there was a heat in his eyes that was new.

"I like it when you touch me."

She hadn't expected him to be vocal, either. She'd always kind of pictured this happening in silence, but his voice brought an extra layer of participation that increased the intimacy between them. "I like it when you touch me, too," she whispered.

"I haven't even started." His hand grazed her breast again. "I'm trying to take it slow for you."

"I won't break," she replied, and hoped it was true.

He smiled then, and reached back under her top. With one hand he flicked the clasp of her bra, setting her breasts free. They felt heavy and needy for his touch, and when he slid his hands beneath the freed bra and filled his palms, she sighed with pleasure.

A few moments later, he reached for the hem of her shirt. "Okay?" he asked, seeking consent for every move. Damn, it was sexy of him to do that. She blocked out the sight of her scars in her mind and nodded her head. She wanted him so much, and wanted to be brave. She didn't want to demand darkness so he wouldn't see, so she could hide. If he was going to be with her, he would have to be with all of her.

The shirt slid easily over her shoulders, and her hair fell down her back as he pulled the fabric—and her bra—away.

There was no going back now. He could see everything.

Burke closed the space between them until his chest brushed against her sensitive breasts, and he dipped his head to kiss her. "You are so beautiful," he whispered, and then he did the most amazing thing. He abandoned her lips and instead bent his head and kissed her shoulder and the puckered skin there.

She'd been telling the truth when she said there was numbness with many of her scars. But numbness didn't mean she couldn't feel at all. She could feel the heat of his lips, the wetness of his tongue as he traced the angry lines. Somehow he was making the thing she hated about herself the most into something erotic and beautiful. Tears pricked behind her eyes as she realized she was in real danger here. A woman could fall in love with a man like Burke Phillips. And that was scary as hell.

His mouth drifted south, away from her scars to her breasts, and desire shot to her core. "Burke," she said hoarsely. "I'm not going to be able to stand up much longer."

His answer was to lift her up and plunk her on the counter, which was very much to his advantage as he stepped into the vee of her legs. His head was now at the perfect height to continue what he'd been doing, and Bella braced her hands on the counter and tried not to rush anything. Except now she was getting anxious, and her body was demanding more even as it was overwhelmed with sensation.

"Come here," he said, and he slid her off the counter so she was straddling his hips. He carried her that way to his bedroom, kicking the door shut with his foot and then taking her to the bed.

Once she was on the covers he reached for the button on his pants and slid them off, standing in front of her now in blue boxer briefs. She wasn't the only one ready for the next step, and Bella undid her trousers and shimmied out of them, with only a tiny scrap of lingerie now between them.

This was going to happen. She was ready. It was the right time, and the right person. It was okay if it hurt for a minute. She told herself all of these things as Burke reached for her panties and gave them a gentle tug.

She'd thought it would happen now, but Burke apparently had different ideas and she could not fault him for his attention to foreplay. He touched, kissed and stroked until she was so wired she wasn't sure what to do with herself. When she was sure she couldn't take another moment, he got a condom out of the nightstand. He peeled off his shorts and put it on before joining her again on the bed.

"Okay?" he asked.

She was terrified. This was the moment. And if he put it off any longer she might actually explode, so she answered, "Mm-hmm."

There was a brief pain, but nothing like she'd expected, and when she looked up Burke was watching her with that intense heat in his eyes that made her feel both powerful and possessed. He didn't look away, either, as he moved, and her heart lurched as she realized that this wasn't just having sex. It was making love. Burke was making love to her and it felt so good and so scary and so right she thought she might die from it.

She moved her hips and his lashes fluttered slightly. She tried it again and he made a sound in his throat that sounded—she hoped—like pleasure. Together they found a rhythm, twined together, and Bella forgot about everything she'd been afraid of, simply getting lost in the sublime sensations taking over her body. She ground against him, seeking some sort of release from the tension coiling in her, and he picked up the pace, until Bella threw her head back on the pillow and called out. She had absolutely no control over the contractions happening, and apparently Burke liked it because he said her name roughly before climaxing.

She'd done it. She was no longer a virgin, and she didn't think Burke had been able to tell. And yet the milestone paled in comparison to the feelings inside her right now for the man holding her in his arms.

She'd gone and done the most predictably teenage thing possible.

She'd fallen in love with the first man she'd slept with.

# CHAPTER NINE

BURKE WASN'T SURE he'd ever be the same again.

Bella lay on his bed, head on his pillow, dark hair every which way. She was delightfully naked, which was a treat for his eyes. His gaze slid briefly over her scars. He didn't give a damn about them and wished she didn't, either. And yet he understood, and he also understood that this was her body and she was the one who got to decide what she did with it.

That she'd chosen to share it with him tonight had been a gift. A gift so great he wasn't sure he could feel his legs yet.

"Hey, Bel?" He looked at her and smiled, his body so blissed out he was sure he looked utterly goofy. "I figured out my theme song."

"Oh?" She looked supremely satisfied.

"Yep. 'Feels Like the First Time' by Foreigner."

Her face blanked and she sat up. "You could tell? Dammit!"

He slid to the side of the bed, alarmed by her quick shift of mood. "Wait, what?"

They stared at each other.

"Never mind," she said.

But her reaction had been so sudden and severe that the seed of an idea was planted in his mind. "What did you mean, I could tell?"

Her cheeks flushed a deep red. "It's nothing. Forget I said anything."

Had this…was it possible that this had been her very first time? He didn't want to be obvious and look for blood, and besides, that didn't always happen anyway. He was more shaken by the emotional consequences of it. Had Bella hidden away all this time? Had she been a virgin… and then she'd finally chosen him?

It was a massive thing, a first time, and he tried not to panic. He kept his voice deliberately and carefully soft as he looked at her. "Bel, if I'd known, I would have been… I don't know. Gentler." Her eyes filled with tears and he felt awful. "I'm sorry," he added.

"No, it's not that. I'm just…humiliated. I didn't want you to know. I hoped you couldn't tell."

Oh, hell. He got up and went to the bathroom briefly, then returned and put his briefs back on. Then he curled up beside her and gathered her into his arms. "The song…that was for me, sweetheart," he said. "Being with you was amazing for me. I honestly didn't know. Did I hurt you?"

She shook her head quickly. "No. And you

didn't need to be gentler, Burke. It was…" She swallowed, and her voice lowered. "It was perfect."

"You're sure? I wish you had told me."

She snorted. "Yeah, right. Thirty years old. And then you would have been worried the whole time. I never wanted you to know. I'm an idiot for reacting as I did."

"No, you're not an idiot. Never." But he had to admit she was right. If he'd known beforehand, it probably would have changed things. He would have worried about whether he was going too fast, about hurting her, about any number of things. "I meant it when I said I couldn't tell. I was just caught up in being with you."

"I'm glad."

"Bella, look at me."

She turned her face up to his and he grazed her cheekbone with his thumb. "I don't want you to have any regrets about tonight. So if there's something you need, please tell me."

"Just hold me for a little while."

That was easy enough to do. He'd asked her to spend the night and they had until dawn. If it was reassurance she needed, he'd give it. It was the least he could do.

And he'd ignore the tinny sound of alarm bells ringing in his head. It shouldn't make a difference, her being a virgin before tonight. He still couldn't believe it. He liked her a lot. Cared for her, certainly. But this was a Big Deal. And he was deathly afraid she was going to experience a level of attachment he wasn't prepared for and certainly hadn't anticipated. Or worse—that he'd start feeling that attachment. That he'd fall for her. Completely and utterly. After tonight, it was a distinct possibility. What had been getting to know each other and fooling around was suddenly very serious. After all his attempts to keep his personal relationships at arm's length, somehow Bella had sneaked past all his defenses in one single day.

He pulled down the covers and invited her to slide beneath the sheets, then opened his arm so she could lie close beside him. She snuggled in, and felt so right with her warm body next to his. She sighed and her muscles relaxed, and his jaw tightened. The protective feelings running through him right now sat uncomfortably in his bones.

"Better?" he asked. He wanted to make sure she was all right but although he'd never been the kind of man to get up and leave after sex, tonight he felt that urge for the first time. Not because he didn't care, but because he found himself caring too much and a sense of self-preservation had kicked in. What was he going to do?

"You didn't mind about my scars?" she asked, her voice small.

He put his own scrambled feelings aside and

turned his full attention to her. "I've never cared, beyond caring that you were hurt so badly. I'm not repulsed. If anything, they show how strong you are."

"Burke…"

He closed his eyes. This was so unexpected, the feelings of tenderness running through him. How he could feel them and still want to flee was troubling. Baffling. The only thing he could come up with was that Bella was different somehow.

God, he didn't need this.

She shifted her head and looked up at him. "Are you all right?" she asked.

"Fine, I'm fine," he answered, smiling down at her.

But he wasn't fine. He was always in control. Always knew exactly what he was doing and what the next step was. He thought he'd known with Bella but then everything had changed. Not because of her scars or because he was her first, though that did hold its own bit of gravity. It was because making love to her had been…profound. It hadn't just felt good, hadn't just filled a physical need, but it had reached into his soul and touched something.

Great. Now he was becoming a poet.

"It's all good, I promise," he said, wanting to reassure her. She deserved that. So he held her closer, wondering what he was going to do in the morning, in the light of day. He didn't want to hurt her. He'd thought they'd been two mature people accepting a night together, acknowledging a connection and acting on it, then going back to their previously scheduled lives with a nice memory. Instead he was in way deeper than he'd ever thought possible. He didn't see a way out of this that didn't involve hurting her.

Hurting someone he cared about.

He was no better than his father.

Bella closed her eyes and let the warm, firm wall that was Burke surround her.

She might not get the chance again, after all. Once he'd discovered she'd been a virgin, he'd definitely tensed up. If only she'd kept her mouth shut when he'd named that stupid song. She sighed, trying to commit every sensation to memory. She wouldn't let what had happened after ruin what had been so amazing before. Sex was definitely not overrated. And sex with Burke…she'd had no idea she could feel that way.

Perhaps she should be embarrassed by how her body had taken over, how she'd sounded—had she really called out his name?—how she'd let herself lose control. But she wasn't. It had been amazing. Nothing could take that away from her.

His fingers traced small circles on her arms in the quiet darkness. Maybe he wanted to sleep, but she wanted to stay awake so she didn't miss a single minute of being in his bed. She let her fingers glide over his chest, touching the warm skin and the sparse, coarse hair at the top of his chest. It rose and fell with his even breathing, and she didn't want to look up to see if he was looking at her or not. She was shy now that the passion had cooled, and she'd never taken the lead with a man before. Even now, she wasn't sure she was ready to start something. Burke's subtle withdrawal had been disappointing, but he'd still pulled her close. It didn't mean he wanted this to happen again. He was too much of a gentleman to turn her away now, wasn't he?

She closed her eyes and told herself to stop putting herself down. What he'd said was that it had been amazing. That he'd been caught up in her. Burke was a lot of things, but she didn't think he was a liar.

Maybe it had taken him by surprise.

Her fingers trailed over a pebbled nipple and his breath caught…he was awake. Bella bit on her lip and kept moving her hand, touching the taut skin over his ribs, the flatness of his stomach, up his strong forearm to his elbow.

"Bella," he murmured.

"Is this okay? I mean, if you'd rather I didn't…"

He let out a sigh. "It feels good. You feel good."

Her heart leaped. Her arm brushed over the covers and discovered that it did indeed feel good when her hand bumped up against his erection. "Oh," she murmured.

"Bella, wait. I need to say something."

She hesitated and looked up. He was gazing down at her with dark, serious eyes, just visible in the light coming through the curtains. Dread spiraled in her. He didn't look like a man ready to ravish her again. He looked like someone about to impart bad news.

Well, she'd handle it. She always did. And thank God she hadn't blurted out her feelings earlier.

"Go ahead," she encouraged.

He sat up a bit, and she nudged herself into a semi-reclining position with the sheets tucked under her armpits. "I think we need to talk about expectations. I love being with you, I do. Today was wonderful. I had such a good time, and I care about you a lot—"

Ugh. Care. She was about to be friend-zoned, wasn't she?

"Being with you…it was so good. And I want to again." His gaze was so magnetic, looking down at her with such seriousness. "But you also deserve to know that I'm not ready for a serious relationship. My life isn't cut out for it, really. I work a million hours and I have ambitions. There are opportunities coming up that I don't want to miss. It doesn't leave a lot of time for nurturing a meaningful relationship."

"I know about a busy job, Burke. I work fifty-or sixty-hour weeks most weeks." Still, she wouldn't have let it keep her from pursuing something she'd considered worthy.

"Right. And I live here in London, and you're in Paris most of the time."

Bella thought of her brother and sister, both of whom had faced the same argument and overcome it. Because they'd loved their partners. Bella thought she felt that way about Burke, too. But if he didn't feel the same, he was right. It wouldn't work.

Her heart threatened to break into pieces. This was the first time she'd allowed herself to be so vulnerable and open with anyone, and now she was starting to feel pushed aside.

"Is this because I…" Oh, it sounded ridiculous to even say it. "Because I'm so inexperienced?"

He shifted and cupped her chin in his hand. "No. I promise you, no. This is my fault, Bella. I've never done serious relationships. I've always been so focused on my career path. And I thought I could do that here, too. That we were similar people of a similar age and that we had a lot in common but it wouldn't get…" His voice trailed away, as his brow wrinkled.

"Messy."

"Right."

"And you think it could."

"I just want to be clear and honest with you. I don't want to hurt you for the world."

She shook her head slightly, removing her chin from his touch. "And this would also manage my expectations."

The conversation had been a complete desire killer. Bella hoped she wasn't showing her emotions on her face, because she was disappointed and feeling like what had started as the most perfect night of her life was now very not. Much like a balloon after the party, when all the air started to leak out and it became a sad, limp version of itself.

"That's not how I'd have chosen to put it," he admitted. "It sounds manipulative and I don't want that. Maybe we should have talked about this beforehand."

"Maybe we should have."

"Would you have changed your mind about staying?"

She stopped and thought. Looked into his face and saw the same man who'd walked through the butterfly house with her today, the same man who'd made sure she'd eaten when her mom was having her procedure, the one who'd held her hand in the park and said nothing for long minutes, the silence comfortable. He'd wanted her, but he didn't want a relationship. Even if she'd known it then, she would have made the same decision. He was being honest now, so how could she fault him? He was a good man, she knew that. And she wouldn't trade what had been between them for anything.

"No," she answered, her voice surprisingly firm. "No, I wouldn't have changed my mind."

"I didn't expect that kind of answer."

"Let me ask you, then. If you had known I was a virgin, would you have changed your mind about asking me?"

He shook his head. "No."

"I might be inexperienced, Burke, but I'm worldly enough to know that a night together doesn't automatically end up as a committed relationship."

It stung to say it, only because she'd fallen for him, big-time. Not just because of the sex, but because of who he was and how he'd treated her over the past weeks. Today she'd imagined, for the first time, what it would be like to have someone in her corner. To have him beside her. How foolish was she?

"I feel like the world's biggest idiot," he admitted.

"Don't. You shouldn't feel stupid for sharing your feelings and your expectations," she said, and meant it. "Fewer misunderstandings that way. Too bad we can't rewind a few hours and have this talk then, you know?"

He chuckled. "I thought about it. I didn't want to kill the vibe. You're very sexy, Arabella."

And there it was. That flicker that brought the flame of her desire to life again. As long as she understood that this night was probably their only night, as long as she managed her own expectations and didn't let her heart get overly involved, tonight didn't need to be over.

"Likewise," she replied, pushing the misgivings aside and embracing the opportunity before her. "And you're a devilishly good kisser."

His lips curved in a smile, though shadows seemed to still lurk behind his eyes. "We're okay?"

She nodded, still disappointed but letting her logical brain take over. Nothing he'd said was incorrect or illogical. "We're okay." Bravado had her adding, "We could be more than okay, if you wanted." She wasn't ready for the night to be over yet.

He reached for her and pulled her close. It was a gorgeous feeling, having only the sheets and his skin against hers. No barriers. No shyness, not anymore. There wasn't room for it.

"You're beautiful," he murmured, burying his face in her hair.

She didn't need his compliments, but it touched her just the same. His hand ran under her hair, sliding along the jagged scar on her neck, but she didn't mind. Not with Burke. And she'd parse all those feelings tomorrow, or the next day. But not now. Now she just wanted to feel this way for as long as she could.

And this time she wanted to play a more active part, explore a little and see if she could make him as weak and pliant as he'd made her. So she reached under the sheets for him, and smiled a wicked little smile as his eyes closed and he groaned.

If they only had one night, it would be one to remember.

# CHAPTER TEN

AURORA WAS IN good spirits when they arrived shortly before eleven. She was waiting for Dr. Mallick to sign her release papers, and then she and Bella would head back to the manor house for a few days of rest before Bella left for Paris.

Bella kissed her mother's cheek and asked about her night, while constantly aware that probably within the next hour she'd be leaving the hospital and Burke would be staying and that would be the end of that. No wedding to bring them together or medical emergency to keep them that way. They were going back to their previously scheduled lives. Without each other. The hope that had spiraled through her yesterday was absent today, leaving a dull ache in its wake. She couldn't fault him one bit for his logic. They did have demanding jobs in different countries. But she also got the feeling there was something else holding him back. It had been behind his eyes last night. And perhaps that was what bothered her the most. She'd shared so much with him, made herself vulnerable, trusted him. That he was keeping something from her hurt. So maybe this was for the best, as much as it stung.

Burke had checked in with the nurses' desk and now he entered the room, his smile relaxed and warm. Bella figured all his patients probably swooned a little when he turned that smile on them, and his warm, magnetic eyes. A stab of pain seemed to center just below her ribs. She wouldn't see that smile again for a very long time.

"Burke. You didn't have to check on me, too." Aurora beamed at him.

"Of course I did. Everything looks great. You make sure you attend your follow-up appointments, too. Dr. Mallick will want to monitor your medications."

"Don't worry. We'll make sure she follows instructions to the letter." Bella said it firmly, while pinning her mother with a stare. Aurora scowled. She was used to giving orders, not taking them, but Bella knew how to bully her into it. "You did promise me yesterday, Maman."

"I knew I'd regret that," Aurora said, but she smiled a little anyway.

"I should leave you to it, then," Burke said. He went to Aurora and gave her a hug. "Glad you're looking and feeling better," he said.

"Thanks to you."

"Not even a little," he replied.

"I'll walk you out," Bella said, keeping her voice light. The last thing Bella needed was her mother asking intrusive questions that she didn't want to answer.

The corridor wasn't much more private, and Bella's stomach churned as she prepared herself for Burke to walk away. Everything he had said last night made perfect sense—to her head. To her heart, not so much. His honesty was hard to fault. They could have this crazy attraction and he was still allowed to not be in a place for a serious relationship. The truth was far better than leading her on, making her believe in possibilities that didn't exist. Deep down, she appreciated his candor.

But her feelings were her own, and real, and to say she wouldn't feel massive disappointment when he left would be a total lie.

"Thank you for everything," she said quietly, squaring her shoulders and forcing herself to meet his gaze. She wouldn't cower. And she wouldn't let him know how hurt she was, either. She and her pride were good friends and had been for many years.

"Bella…"

"No, Burke." She inhaled and let it out again. She was tempted to ask him what else was bothering him. What was keeping him from sharing his heart with her, because she couldn't escape the feeling he was hiding something. But this was neither the time nor the place. "Not here, and not when it won't make any difference. We had an amazing time. Now we need to go back to our regular lives, that's all."

"I hurt you. When you get all practical like this, I can tell. God, Bella, I'm sorry."

She didn't want to make herself more vulnerable, so she shrugged. It took all of her energy to make that one simple movement nonchalant. "If my feelings got a little hurt, so what? I'll get over it. For God's sake, we only spent one night together. I'm stronger than that."

Now *he* looked hurt, which made no sense at all since he'd been the one to state in no uncertain terms that a relationship was off the table.

"You're the strongest woman I know," he said, his damnable dark eyes searching hers.

"See?" She smiled. "Look, you made last night better than I could have hoped or imagined, so let's just leave it at that." That much was at least true.

"As long as you're all right."

A lump formed in her throat and she ignored it. "I'm always all right," she answered. Then, because standing there with him was torture, she rose on tiptoe and kissed his cheek, breathing in his cologne for the last time. "I should get Maman ready to go. Goodbye, Burke."

He nodded, looked as if he might say something, and then reconsidered. Finally he managed, "Bye, Bella."

She turned around and walked back into the hospital room, schooling her features. She was good at that, after years of practice. And it was far better for her to do the walking away than to watch him leave.

Aurora was sitting up in bed, sipping on the cup of juice left from her breakfast. One look at Bella and she put the cup down on her tray and frowned. She swore in French—something Bella hadn't heard in quite some time—and sighed.

"I am grateful to Burke for helping me, but I could kill him for hurting you."

Bella stopped short and gaped at her mother. "What?"

"I've seen that look many times, *ma petite*. That look right there, on your face, pretending nothing is wrong and that you don't care. I saw it nearly thirteen years ago when you were dying for his attention and he acted as if you didn't exist."

Bella sank down on the end of the bed and let out a massive breath. "How did you…" After a pause, she met her mother's gaze. "I never told anyone about my crush on him."

"Mothers see things. And understand. And you are stubborn like me, my darling. I knew long ago that you got into that car that night because you wanted to show Burke you didn't care about him. Or at least I suspected. In the years since, you have avoided him completely, until the wedding. It all made sense to me. But when I saw you together, I hoped he'd finally realize what a treasure you are. And now he's gone and hurt you."

Bella absorbed all of that information—apparently she wasn't as good at hiding her feelings as she thought—and took a moment to think about how to respond. Aurora waited. Bella had the thought that maybe her mother understood more than she had ever given her credit for. Bella had been missing her dad so much that maybe she'd lost sight of how amazing her remaining parent really was.

"You could tell all that from me walking in the room." It was a statement, not a question.

"You are a master at pretending everything is fine. So am I. Like recognizes like, you know."

Bella was determined not to cry. Her mother was right—they were both strong women who had been through significant challenges in their lives. "In Italy, I got to know him better. He's a good man, Maman. And he has been so good to you. Yesterday was the most amazing day. And yes, I got my hopes up. But Burke is not interested in anything serious. He's married to his job. This morning he told me about an opportunity coming up at the Royal Brompton & Harefield that would make his entire career. He has ambitions. And a love life is not top of his list."

"Perhaps you can change his mind."

Bella dug in her heels. "Maman. I do not want to have to make anyone 'change their mind' or be convinced. Call me naive, or a foolish romantic, but if someone wants to be with me badly enough they will. I'm not prepared to compete with a career for snippets of attention."

"Your father had to compete with my career."

"For your time, maybe. But not for love. And that's a big difference."

"*Oui, ma petite*. It is. I'm glad you realize it, but sorry that you are in that position." She reached out and took Bella's hand. "It is a shame. It's so obvious he cares for you."

"It is." Bella fought back the stinging in her eyes and the tightening in her throat. "But we are adults who know what we want. Truthfully, I wouldn't trade the last few weeks even though I ended up being vulnerable. I learned some valuable lessons."

Aurora lifted a perfectly shaped eyebrow. "Such as?"

"Such as my scars maybe aren't as repulsive as I think they are. That at least one person saw them and didn't care at all. Still told me I was beautiful. That counts for something, right?"

Aurora frowned. "Now I do want to kill him."

Bella laughed. "No, it's not his fault. He's worked so hard to get where he is. I understand. And I have no regrets."

She really didn't. They hadn't argued or said things they would want to take back. She'd spent a wonderful day with a lovely man and felt as beautiful in his arms as she ever had on any red carpet or in any magazine. There had been nothing casual or flippant about it. He hadn't lied to her, not once.

"So what next?"

"Next we get you out of here and back home. We cater to your every whim. You answer any questions I have as I take over the reins for a while, and when I'm sure you're doing all right, I head back to Paris and the office. Everything just as we planned."

Aurora leaned forward and kissed Bella's forehead. "You stand at the back of the Pemberton line too often, Arabella. But I think you might just be the strongest of all of us."

It didn't feel that way, but she absorbed the compliment as it was intended. She was strong. She was resilient. And the only way to go on was forward. Even if her heart was, if not broken, cracked a little.

The doctor came in for one last check and then finally Aurora was released to go home. Their driver was waiting when they exited the hospital into the brisk summer air, and stowed their small bags in the back. It seemed no time at all and they were weaving through the city, heading toward home.

"Are you tired?" Bella asked.

"Actually, no. I feel surprisingly well. A little sore perhaps." She looked down at her lap. "A bit around the site where they put the catheter in. And a little tenderness here." She put her hand on her chest.

"But the doctor said those are normal."

"And should go away in another day or so." Aurora smiled. "I know I said I'd let you baby me, so I won't tell you not to fuss. But I do feel better."

Bella had to admit that before the procedure there'd been a strained look around her mother's eyes. She hadn't really noticed until now, when it was gone. She would always have Burke to thank for that. Aurora might have not sought medical help otherwise.

When they arrived at Chatsworth Manor, Mrs. Flanagan greeted them at the door and ushered them in. She'd been absent when they'd first arrived after the wedding, off sick for a few days. The house had felt strange in her absence.

"Maggie," Aurora said, squeezing her arm. "It's so good to see you. You're feeling better?"

"Much, thank you. And it's good to see you, too, looking so well. The procedure was clearly a success?" She formed it as a question.

"Very," Bella said, leaning forward and kissing their housekeeper's cheek. In reality, the woman was very much like a second mother to her. "How's Esme?"

"Well, thanks. Working at the inn still." Mrs. Flanagan's daughter was the same age as Stephen. She'd married once, but after a few years they'd divorced. Bella had never understood. Esme was a beautiful, warm, funny woman. "Anyway," Mrs. Flanagan added, "enough about my family. We've got everything ready for you, madame."

As familiar as the family was with the long-time servants, Mrs. Flanagan always called Aurora "madame."

"Would you like tea, Maman? I can put our things upstairs and we can have tea in the library. You didn't eat lunch and only had hospital food last night and this morning."

"I could eat," Aurora admitted.

"I'll have tea and sandwiches in twenty minutes," Mrs. Flanagan promised, and whisked away.

Bella saw her mother to the library and then took both their bags upstairs to their rooms. She dropped Aurora's bag inside and left it for Aurora to unpack…not that she wouldn't help, but she did respect her mother's right to privacy and unpacking a few items wouldn't tax her unnecessarily.

Then she went to her room, stood inside the

door, and let the feelings of the past three hours wash over her.

This was what her family never understood and never saw.

She leaned against her door and dropped her head, letting out a long, shaky breath. Her heart ached. Her body ached in places she had ignored until just this moment, when she was alone and felt free enough to acknowledge the discomfort.

What she had felt for Burke—what she still felt for him—wasn't because he'd been the first and only man she'd ever had sex with. It certainly cemented her feelings in her heart, but it went far deeper than that, to compassion and acceptance. She'd waited long enough. Last night she'd wanted him to say different words. Wanted him to say "let's give this a go" and maybe, just maybe, fall in love. She was already there; all he had to do was catch up.

To have that gift sitting right in front of her and then snatched away again was devastating. She could pretend all she wanted in front of Burke, her mother, her family…but inside, she was so very hurt. He cared about her, but not enough. He trusted her, but not completely. His answers had been too pat, too perfect, too logical. And he'd avoided her eyes several times this morning. It was unlike him, so why?

And did it matter? Thinking about it didn't change a thing.

She dropped her bag on the floor and left it rather than unpacking. She gave herself five minutes to feel and wallow and let down her guard. Then she went to her bathroom and splashed water on her face, and redid her makeup in the way that covered her blemishes and still made her look fresh and dewy—well, as dewy as a thirty-year-old could look, she supposed. Then she gave her head a shake and set her lips. Women could be dewy at thirty! Just because she was feeling old right now didn't mean she was.

And if Burke could find her attractive, someone else could, too. Maybe it was time she stopped hiding away. The idea felt revolutionary. And not something she should rush into, but it was something worth exploring. Maybe talking with Maman. Or Charlotte. Whatever she did would ripple down into the company, as well. She would never make a big decision without considering the family and Aurora Inc.

"Time," she murmured to her reflection in the mirror. "Take your time, Bella." She knew herself well enough to know she was being a bit reactive to Burke's rejection. Honestly, the whole thing about someone else finding her attractive was a bit moot anyway. She didn't want anyone else. At least not now.

But the feeling of needing to stop hiding persisted as she made her way back downstairs to the library.

She arrived just after the tea had been delivered and poured a cup for Aurora and herself. Aurora took a splash of milk; Bella left hers black and took a chair at an angle to her mother. The tea was hot and revivifying, and she let out a happy sigh. Almost every problem she could remember had been tackled by ordering tea first.

Mrs. Flanagan had brought an assortment of sandwiches as well, and Bella's stomach growled in response to the sight and smell of them. "Sandwich, Maman?" she asked.

"I could nibble. Especially if that's Marjorie's bread. No one makes bread like her."

The cook had been with the family for well over a decade. Her bread was soft and fragrant, and she'd made one of Maman's favorites: turkey with cranberry and provolone. Bella bit into it and the flavors melted on her tongue. This—the sandwiches and tea—was the taste of home.

"Maman, may I talk to you about something? It affects the company in a roundabout way, and I want to get your feedback on it."

Aurora put down the tea. "Of course, darling. What is it?"

"I've been thinking a lot about how I've, well, hidden since my accident. Some of that has been personal. A lot of it has been personal." She sighed. "Oh, hell. Most of it has been. But I do realize that anything I do trickles down into the company, and by extension the rest of the family."

"And as the person who holds it all together, the last thing you want to do is be the cause of a problem."

As usual, her mother nailed it. "Well, yes. I mean, our personal lives are always fodder for the press. When Dad died..." Her throat tightened. "And then Stephen's engagement, and Gabi leaving him at the altar, and her falling for William...and then the sabotage in New York and Charlotte's very quick wedding. I do not want to be the cause of more—I guess salacious is the word I'm looking for—speculation in the tabloids."

Aurora lifted her teacup again. "This is about your scars, yes?"

Bella nodded, feeling somewhat miserable. Once she'd listed off everything that had happened, she realized that if she went public with her scars, she'd be contributing to a lot of stress the family had felt over the past few years.

"They are your scars. Whether you hide them or show them is your personal decision. Don't worry about the company. What's important is you. This has always been your decision to make."

Resentment flickered through Bella's chest for a moment. At eighteen, once she'd healed, she'd been left with the decision to how to deal with her disfigurement. She knew her parents had wanted to respect her wishes, but looking back she wondered if it wouldn't have been better if they'd told her she couldn't hide them or pretend they didn't exist. If they'd guided—parented—a little more rather than letting her make that choice all alone at a time when she was trying to come to grips with it herself.

But she wouldn't say that to Maman. One, she'd just had a heart procedure, and two, it wouldn't change anything now. Deep down she knew that her mother and father had done what they thought was the right, caring thing. She could never fault them for that.

"I don't know what I want," she admitted. "I'm just starting to feel like I've been living… I don't know. Not a lie, exactly, but not the truth, either. And certainly not living fully."

"Has being with Burke brought this on? This reexamination of what you want your life to look like?"

"Maybe. And we're not together. We're not going to be together. But the times we were… they were so lovely, and different, and he'd already seen my scars before the wedding and it didn't make a difference to him. But Maman, I don't want to be plastered all over the media, either."

"Unless you do it on your terms." Aurora finished her tea and got up to pour more. "Even the hardest things in the world are made easier when we take ownership of them."

"I don't want to negatively affect the business. We've promoted a message of 'everyone is beautiful' but this whole time I've been wearing long sleeves and my hair down and keeping this big ugly secret. I feel like a massive hypocrite."

"Why don't you talk to Charlotte? She's still managing PR and she loves you. If you're ready, she can help you craft something that respects you and is a positive for the company as well. It's not about avoiding the fallout, Bella. It's about managing it. And our family is strong and resilient. The past months have shown that."

"But for how long?" Bella asked.

Aurora was silent for a long moment, and then she looked at Bella straight in the eye. "I understand that your concern is genuine, but I think you need to ask yourself if this worry over the business is an excuse to hold you back so you don't have to do the hard thing."

That stung. Not because it was a baseless accusation but because it was entirely possible that Bella had done exactly that. How many times had she envied her sister her strapless and backless gowns, her sweeping updos, but told herself it was for the good of the company? Really she had been protecting herself so long it had become her only way of life. In every part of her life.

"I'm sorry, *ma petite*. I don't mean to hurt you. But if you're considering this, I think it needs to be said. Aurora Inc. will survive. You can't hide behind it anymore."

Nerves tangled in Bella's stomach, mixing with fear. And yet she was tired of not being herself. She thought back to a mere twenty-four hours ago, when she'd been enjoying the afternoon with Burke, just being Bella. She'd put her hair up, not caring if he saw the scar. She'd had dinner with him. She'd made love to him, with all of her scars on display, and they'd meant nothing. He'd kissed them as if they were cherished. He'd seen her pain and honored it.

And she'd felt seen and heard and beautiful. Maybe they didn't have a future together, but he'd given her that wonderful gift just the same.

"I need to think about it more. But thank you, Maman, for the hard truths. I needed to hear them."

"Finish your sandwich," Aurora commanded. "You need to look after yourself. And so do I. We're stronger than most give us credit for, Bella. Remember that."

Bella picked up the sandwich and ate despite the unease and anxiety centered in her belly. This week she'd work with Maman here at the house, and then she'd be back in Paris. Once there, maybe she would talk to Charlotte.

# CHAPTER ELEVEN

AFTER NEARLY THREE weeks away from her flat, Bella was glad to be home again. Her apartment was in the Seventh Arrondissement, with a view of the lush building courtyard rather than the Eiffel Tower. With several windows and lovely light wood floors throughout, the space felt more airy and spacious than it was. But it was more than enough for her. Three bedrooms, two baths and a spacious living room was more than enough for a single person. Sometimes it was too much, when she was here alone, but she loved it just the same.

Charlotte was staying over for a few days before heading back to London. It gave the team a chance to have a full in-person attendance meeting, and it meant Bella could talk to her about her thoughts. Though she missed having Charlotte in the city all the time, the benefit to having her live with Jacob in Richmond was having her here to stay when she was in town.

Bella was in the kitchen cooking, making one

of her personal favorites for dinner, salmon *en croûte*. Charlotte would be along soon, and the salmon with salad would make a lovely dinner for them both. She hummed tunelessly as she wrapped the salmon in the whisper-thin pastry, then brushed the top with egg wash. Cooking was also something she'd missed. Gabi's mother had done most of the cooking during the visit to the Baresis, and since then the staff at the manor house had kept her well-fed.

Charlotte knocked on the door and Bella wiped her hands on a towel before going to answer. When she opened it, Charlotte stepped inside carrying a stylish overnight bag and a paper sack from her favorite bakery.

"You brought dessert."

"I did. You're going to feed me something healthy. Which is great. My obstetrician will be pleased. But sometimes I need sugar."

Bella grinned sheepishly. It was also true that she was glad to be back as she had been on the treadmill the last two mornings, bright and early. She'd missed her morning exercise.

"Not too healthy. Salmon wrapped in pastry."

"Oh, yum. The kind you make with the lemon-butter sauce?"

"That's the one. Come in and have a drink."

Bella poured wine for herself and sparkling water for Charlotte, then added a slice each of lemon and lime to liven it up a bit. Charlotte was looking radiant, with her rounded tummy and the glow in her cheeks. Pregnancy suited her.

"You look wonderful," Bella said, admiring her sister's flair for style as her body made room for the new life she was carrying. Today she wore a sleeveless maxi dress in blue with pink flowers, with the pleated bust forming a fashionable knot in the center. Yesterday she'd worn a T-shirt dress that had conformed to her figure, and the sky-high heels she adored. Charlotte wasn't interested in hiding her baby bump at all.

"I feel wonderful. The second trimester is much better than the first," she admitted, taking a drink of her water. "Honestly, the hormones work in Jacob's favor." She winked at Bella, and Bella laughed.

"Ew! TMI, Charlotte."

"Whatever. I figured if I led with that, you'd tell me what happened with you and Burke."

Heat rushed into Bella's cheeks, and not because she opened the oven to slip the salmon inside. "Hmm. Nosy, nosy."

"You're my sister. I saw how it was in Italy. And on the flight back. What happened in London? Anything juicy?"

Bella couldn't look at her sister. Instead she went to work making the sauce for the fish. As she put ingredients in her blender, she affected a shrug. "Oh, you know."

"Bella!"

In response Bella turned on the blender, drowning out any potential conversation. She was going to tell Charlotte. She was going to tell her sister a lot of things, but she was still going to make Charlotte work for it. After all, that was what siblings did.

When the blender shut off, Charlotte pinned her with a glare. "Funny," she said, pointing at Bella. "Something did happen. Out with it."

"You're very bossy."

"This is not news."

Bella laughed despite herself. Then she sobered. It was hard, letting herself be vulnerable, even with those who loved her best. "I spent the night at his flat while Maman was in the hospital."

Charlotte's eyes got huge and she smiled triumphantly. "I knew it! Oh, Bella, he's so hunky."

Bella rolled her eyes. "Well, he's also not interested in a relationship, so there's that."

The triumphant smile turned to a frown of disgust. "Then he is a horrible man who foolishly let the best thing to happen to him get away."

It was said partly in jest, but Bella hadn't realized how desperately she'd needed to hear the unconditional support. She put the blender aside and went to sit next to Charlotte on a barstool. "I needed that," she admitted, taking a drink of her wine. "He is hunky, Charlotte. And so wonderful in every other way."

Charlotte put down her glass and turned on the stool so she was facing Bella. "Are you in love with him?"

If Aurora had asked, she would have denied it. But to her sister, she couldn't. "I think I am. It's ridiculous. There was Italy and then London. It was literally two weeks."

Charlotte lifted her hand where the diamond ring sparkled. "Reader, I married him."

Bella burst out laughing. Charlotte always had this dry, funny way of putting things that got right to the heart of the matter. She and Jacob had known each other for nine days and at the end of that time Charlotte was head over heels. If anyone understood what it was like, it was Charlotte. Or even William, for that matter. But Bella wasn't up to discussing this with her brother.

"Did you two...sleep together?"

The coil of anxiety wound tighter in Bella's stomach, but she had to talk to someone. "Yeah. We did." She hesitated and met Charlotte's eyes. Her sister was watching her soberly. Thank God she wasn't making fun or light of anything right now. Bella took a breath and said, "He was my first."

Charlotte's mouth dropped open. Then she sighed and said, "Oh, Bella. I'm sorry."

"Don't be sorry. It was wonderful." Now she wanted to cry, but she wouldn't. "He didn't know.

But even so, he did everything exactly right." Her face was flaming, she was sure of it. "But it made walking away from him a lot harder than it might have been otherwise."

She took another drink of wine. Charlotte reached for the bottle and refilled the glass. "So you regret it?"

"Not a bit. I just wanted more."

"And you're sure he doesn't?"

"He made it very clear. His career is more important right now."

Charlotte scowled and made a sound in the back of her throat. "Chicken," she muttered. "Look," she said louder, "my husband runs a business in London and Aurora is in Paris, but we found a way."

"I know. And so did William and Gabi. But when I think about that, I try to remember that I shouldn't judge Burke by the same yardstick. He was honest with me, Charlotte. Although…"

"Although what?"

Bella frowned. "It's probably stupid, but that morning I just got the feeling that there was more to it than just logistics. But Burke…he's only let me see what he wants me to see. It took me a while to realize it. We all have secrets, I suppose. I can't fault him for that."

"Well, I can." Charlotte got up and went to get the bottle of Perrier. "If he doesn't see how amazing you are, sod him."

A smile crept up Bella's cheek. "I love you for that."

"Of course you do. Bella, you've spent so much time in the background, being the all-round manager of both the family and business. You're the peacemaker when the rest of us stir up trouble. You stepped up for Will when Stephen was being a jerk. You're filling in for Maman. We count on you far too much, but you deserve things for yourself, too." She looked at Bella with a keen expression. "Are you ready to take them?"

This was the opening Bella had been waiting for. "I might be. I wanted to talk to you tonight about doing things differently. One of the reasons I'm not mad at Burke is that he made me see that I don't always have to hide. My scars didn't matter to him. And I got a taste of what that's like… being free of them. What if I stopped hiding behind my hair and long sleeves? What would happen in the publicity department? I don't want to hurt the company."

"The company will survive. We had our new line sabotaged in New York and came out stronger than ever. We had the Will-and-Stephen drama and nothing happened sales-wise. Don't worry about the company. Do what's right for you. And the company—and family—will support you through it."

God bless Charlotte.

The oven dinged, and Bella got up to take the

golden-brown salmon out. She took the salad and vinaigrette out of the fridge and served them both dinner, and then they brainstormed ideas and worked through contingencies until Bella was comfortable with a route forward. Now the only thing to do was bring in the rest of the family—which would happen tomorrow, at the morning meeting.

Later, Charlotte's soft snores came from the guest room, but Bella lay awake late into the night, hoping she was doing the right thing, exhilarated and terrified by turns.

It was going to take a lot of courage on her part, but it was time she stepped into her own.

Burke decided to walk home from work. It was a gorgeous summer evening, which was a change from the fog and drizzle of the morning. He could use the exercise and fresh air to clear his head. It had been a jumbled mess since Bella had turned away from him outside Aurora's room.

He was waiting for his interview at the Royal Brompton and sweating about it. Working there was the opportunity of a lifetime, and came around just about as often. So why was he not focused on that and instead kept thinking about Bella and the night they'd spent together?

He didn't want marriage. He didn't want that battle between his career and family. On the outside, the Phillips family had seemed so wonderful and…cohesive. But Burke knew better. His father had been gone a lot. The days of aristos not having to work for a living were gone. And then Burke had also learned a horrible secret that he'd never shared with his mother. His father had a mistress.

The term sounded so antiquated. Burke had seen them once when he was sixteen. He'd gone to Norwich for a school break with a mate and he'd spied his father in a pub, cozied up with another woman. The shock had been complete. And he'd never told a living soul. Not even his dad. When the family had gone to such trouble to keep Burke's name out of the accident, he'd felt he hadn't the right to drop any sort of bombshell. He'd had his own shame to bear, so how could he fault someone else? After that, every time his father had been away, Burke had wondered if it was actually business or if he was seeing *her*.

But it explained why his mother had spent so much time with them as children, especially the girls. Father had been gone a lot. And she'd done her best to provide a stable, loving upbringing for her kids.

Burke crossed the bridge and the breeze from the Thames lifted his hair and cooled his face. While he couldn't imagine ever cheating on Bella, he had no desire to be caught in between a woman and his work. One or both would suffer because of it. He'd made peace with his single status long ago. So why was it so hard now?

He was nearly home when he stopped at a tiny market for something quick for dinner. He was standing at the checkout waiting to go through when a headline on the cover of a tabloid caught his eye.

*The Not-So-Perfect Pemberton!*

That part was in big font, with smaller print underneath.

*Arabella Germain-Pemberton steps out strapless...and scarred!*

The photo had captured Bella in a strapless black-and-white gown, her hair up, diamonds sparkling at her neck. Burke's heart lurched as he absorbed the sucker punch. She'd done it. She'd gone out in public without hiding. Why? When? He grabbed the cheap paper rag and put it on top of his tikka masala entrée on the checkout belt.

He waited to read until he got home and put the dinner in the microwave to heat. Then he flipped to the page and read it standing at the kitchen counter. Seeing her there, in full color, did something to his insides he didn't quite understand. The photog had captured her from the thighs up, so that the zigzags marking her pale skin were on full display. She was at least smiling, and not scowling or caught in one of those moments where people were speaking and looked awful on tabloid covers. She looked beautiful. Considering how protective she'd been only weeks ago, he couldn't help but be astounded by her bravery.

Without him. Regret slammed into him, not for the first time. Walking away might be for the best, for both of them, but nothing about it had been easy.

According to the article, she'd been out at a charity event for a children's hospital. She'd worn a strapless Aurora design and Aurora diamonds, but the big news was the slashes on her arms, shoulders and neck that had caught everyone's attention. There was great speculation on their origin—how long ago, what had happened. Had she been attacked? Had she been a cutter? The delight that was taken by the journos made him sick to his stomach. They made money off someone else's pain.

He couldn't believe she'd done it. He was in awe of her strength and fortitude, for she'd surely known there'd be a reaction. For a woman who'd never let anyone see her be vulnerable, had never even been with a man before…before… She was extraordinarily brave.

The microwave beeped and he opened the door and then shut it again, so it wouldn't beep constantly. Instead of eating, he retrieved his laptop from his room and put it on the counter, then did an internet search. He was gratified to see that a statement from Aurora was near the top of the results, and that it came from Bella herself.

*Society has this concept of beauty that is impossible to live up to. It would be hypo-critical of me to hide away any longer, not embodying the principles that Aurora holds dear—that every person is beautiful, has their own story, and deserves happiness and acceptance.*

*I have scars. My history may be personal, but it is no reason to hide or try to live a lie of perfection. It's not bodies that make us beautiful, but souls.*

The social media statement ended with a hashtag: *#showyourbeautiful.*

A quick glance at the results showed several hundred results in the past twenty-four hours.

In another twenty-four, he guessed Arabella would go totally viral.

He poured a drink and sat on the sofa. What had possessed her to do such a thing? He was proud of her, so very proud. But also a little bit afraid. He doubted the press would let this go. If they went digging, they'd find out about the accident. And then his name would be brought into it.

The whiskey burned in his throat as he tossed it back and went for another. To say he felt like a hypocrite was an understatement, because he was glad for her but wished she hadn't gone public for his own self-preservation. To criticize her for this would be unconscionable. He'd walked away from the wreckage with a broken arm that had long since healed. He had a blossoming career because he'd tried to use his experience to do good in the world. But if the press went digging, how would a potential employer look at his involvement that night? What if he ended up in the news as well? It wasn't a stretch; he was Viscount Downham. The title alone made him newsworthy. How much fallout would he suffer? Would it affect his future at the Royal Brompton?

He looked at the photo again and felt a longing so intense it frightened him. She hadn't called or texted or anything. Hadn't shared with him, and that was his fault, wasn't it? He was the one who'd sent her away.

He downed the drink and went to eat his dinner, though it took him a while as he mostly picked at it until it was not quite gone. He paced a while in his living room, fixed himself one more drink, let the liquor ease his conscience and bolster his bravery. Dammit, he was calling her.

She didn't answer the phone for several rings, and he was just about to hang up when she finally picked up. "Hello?"

At the sound of her voice he nearly lost his. After three seconds he finally managed, "It's Burke."

There was another three seconds of telling silence. "What can I do for you, Burke?"

"Bella," he chided softly, hurt that she took such a businesslike tone with him. "I just saw the tabloids. I wanted to make sure you're okay."

"I'm fine. It was planned, you know." At least she didn't pretend not to know what he was talking about.

"I figured it was. But…how has the reaction been?"

She sighed. "It's been a lot, sometimes. Some is a lot of support. But that doesn't sell magazines, does it? So there's speculation. I'll weather it. My family is one hundred percent behind me."

"I am, too, Bella. You must know that."

She was silent, and he got the feeling she was measuring her words. When she finally spoke again, she said, "I know you mean well, Burke, and I don't have any hard feelings. But you were clear in what you wanted, which means you don't really have a part in this." Her voice was cool but not unfriendly. Just matter-of-fact. And it cut him to the bone.

"I don't mean to be unkind," she continued. "The time we had together gave me the courage to step forward, and it will always be a good memory for me. But if we aren't going to be a thing, we can't do this."

"What, talk?" he asked, incredulous.

"Yes, talk. I accept everything you said. But

that doesn't mean it didn't hurt. It's just best if we leave it at that, okay?"

He leaned back in his chair and swiped his hand over his face. Was she saying that he'd had the power to really, really hurt her? Yes, it had been her first time, but Bella didn't strike him as the type to go starry-eyed just because of that. She was too pragmatic.

And yet he supposed it was possible, because he'd been moping around here, too, missing her like crazy. He hated the thought of hurting anyone, but most of all Bella. This was why he'd fallen back on charm and stayed away from commitment. He didn't trust himself not to hurt people. If you kept people on the surface, everything was safe. He'd tried to protect her and instead he'd hurt her anyway.

"Have you been asked a lot of questions about what happened, and when?" He changed the subject, wanting to abide by her wishes. No more talk about the two of them.

"Yes. I haven't answered much. I want to focus on the future and not the past. And to be honest, I've been quite busy filling in for Maman. I was just about to leave my office when you called."

"But it's nearly eight."

"Oh, good. An early night for me, then."

She was being so cold, so different from the Bella he knew, and then it finally hit him, made sense. Bella put up walls when she felt too much, didn't she? And she'd said he'd hurt her. He was sorry for that, but glad that she hadn't forgotten him or that he was at least hard to get over. He had no right to want it but it was a tiny bit of comfort just the same.

Truth was, he didn't know what he wanted. To protect himself. To see her again. To stay untethered and free. To love her. Of course, he couldn't say any of those things. "How much longer are you filling in for her?"

"Another few weeks for sure. Then she's going to head to the château for a while. Honestly, I think Maman might semi-retire. Which means lots of changes at Aurora Inc. At least Will is back, but later this fall Charlotte will be on maternity leave."

So she was feeling the pressure of being in the driver's seat. "Please take time for yourself, too," he said softly. "You should take a weekend at the château as well. All work and no play."

"Said the pot to the kettle." Finally her voice warmed. "The hospital is good?"

"Yeah. My meeting at the Royal Brompton is next week. I've been working and prepping."

"Good luck. I know how much it means to you."

It did, really. It was his chance to really move up, to make a name for himself. One that…well, one that hadn't already belonged to someone else. He pinched the top of his nose and let out a breath. Hell. Why had he been thinking about his father so much lately?

"Thanks. I should probably go so you can go home. I'm glad you're okay. I'm glad you did what you did, too. The world deserves to know the real you, Bella."

"Thanks," she replied, her voice soft. "I'll see you."

He said goodbye and then sat there for twenty minutes, wondering if her "I'll see you" was meant to be some sort of code or invitation or if it was simply an alternate way of saying bye.

Either way, saying goodbye hadn't been nearly as easy as he'd wanted it to be. And that bothered him more than a little. He didn't know what to do with it or how to proceed.

The fact remained—she was dedicated to her life at Aurora and he was equally dedicated to his career. And if his parents' marriage had taught him anything, it was that when people weren't dedicated to each other, nothing was worth a damn.

# CHAPTER TWELVE

"THAT WAS HIM, wasn't it?" Charlotte asked Bella.

They were currently in Bella's office, and Charlotte was sitting with her feet up because she was having some swelling in her ankles. Charlotte was now staring at Bella with open curiosity and Bella was trying to sort out her emotions from hearing Burke's voice again.

"It was, yes. He saw a photo. Called to check in."

"Nice of him."

Bella snorted. "That is not what you really want to say."

Charlotte pondered for a moment. "Honestly, I don't know what I want to say. It's clear you care about him. It's also clear that you're standing your ground, which I very much admire."

Standing her ground, huh. She didn't want to admit how miserable she was. Work was fine. A bit overwhelming, but nothing she couldn't handle. Even the charity event and the dress... they'd planned for that and it had been more empowering than she'd imagined. When the gossip started to get to her, she channeled her energies into remembering that feeling, standing on the steps, in the kind of gown she'd always dreamed of wearing.

She'd stepped out of the shadows and into the light. It should have been glorious. Instead she just kept hearing Burke's voice saying he didn't want to be involved. As much as she told herself to be pragmatic and that it was fine, it still hurt. Because her feelings had escalated very quickly, and a man like Burke wasn't easy to forget.

"I'm fine," she insisted, and Charlotte nodded in confirmation.

"Of course you're fine. But fine isn't happy or contented or delirious with love and basking in afterglow."

Bella rolled her eyes. "No one says afterglow anymore."

"They should. Boneless, delicious illumination after mind-blowing sex."

Bella burst out laughing. It was impossible not to love Charlotte. "I'm sorry you're heading back to London tomorrow. I'm going to miss you."

"Me, too, but Jacob is already back and I'm sorry, but…"

"I get it. Spare me the details."

Charlotte got up, curving a hand around her belly as she did so. "Are you sure you don't want to fight for him, Bel? He might be worth it."

"I don't want to have to convince a man to be with me. Then I'd always wonder if he really wanted to be there or if he'd been coerced or cajoled."

"You put on some of the new lingerie line and he could be cajoled, all right. And PS, no one says cajoled anymore, either."

Bella shared a smile with her sister. Charlotte had been the bright spot over the last few weeks, working together, hanging out in the evenings, such as they were. But Bella was going to be alone soon, and she wouldn't be able to pretend or hide from herself.

"His interview is coming up. Charlotte, unless we move the company across the Channel, we can't all just uproot and move to London."

"I know. Especially you. It's easier for me to work remotely."

"Why me?"

"Because you really are the new Aurora. Haven't you figured that out yet? You've stepped in like you were born to it, which you probably were. Ask Stephen if you don't believe me. I mean, your hashtag is going to start a whole new marketing campaign."

It was true. When they'd crafted her statement, and she'd come up with *#showyourbeautiful*, it was like everything fell into place. But the new Aurora? "Maman isn't retiring. So no, I'm not her."

"Don't be so sure. I'm guessing she'd like to be more of a figurehead now. And I think the health scare affected her a lot. Are you prepared to step in?"

She was. Despite the nerves and reservations and long hours, she'd enjoyed the past few weeks a lot. William was back and they'd worked as a collective, but her siblings had all deferred to her judgment. It had given her a confidence that had been missing until now. After years of being steadfastly behind the scenes and working hard, she felt…prepared.

It was the weirdest thing.

They were heading for the elevator when Charlotte asked a bombshell question. "But if Burke came to you right now and asked you to drop everything to be with him, would you?"

She knew she had fallen in love with Burke in London. Knew it without a doubt, deep in her bones. And yet the answer came to her instantly and definitively. "No."

She expected her sister to say something like, "See? If you really loved him, nothing would stand in your way." Charlotte surprised her instead. "Good. Because although I might be pretty new at this—you know, love, marriage—it's a compromise. It's realizing what's important to the other person and coming up with ways to make that happen."

The elevator doors opened and they stepped inside.

"I'm going to miss you, Charlotte."

"I'll be on a video call with you tomorrow."

"It's not the same. Thank you. For the past few weeks, for your love and support and advice. I appreciate it more than you know."

Charlotte smiled and patted her tummy. "I swear it's Jacob. He's made me a big marshmallow."

Bella laughed, but as the elevator doors closed, she realized that Burke had never been further from her. If he wasn't willing to take a step toward compromise, what chance would they ever have? It would be better to put him out of her mind completely.

The next week passed in a blur of meetings, consultations and two very visible social engagements. For the first one, Bella didn't look to make as bold a statement as she had at the children's charity. When she attended a private and lavish fundraiser at the Louvre, where a weekend at the château was an auction item, she chose an Aurora cocktail dress with a sleeveless white silk bodice—plunging to the waist—and an ecru skirt beaded with clear and black crystals. Her shoulders were covered but not her arms, and her hair was done in an elaborate twist and anchored with more crystals.

The second engagement was an album launch by a popular rock band at Le Cabaret Sauvage, and it was an occasion for the more dramatic and daring. For that one she chose something unlike anything she'd worn before. She didn't want to be a carbon copy of her mother, who always dressed with class and elegance. Bella was only thirty, after all. She wore a long gold-sequined gown with thin spaghetti straps that crossed in the back and a deep slit that ran from hip to ankle.

The magazines went crazy, their covers shouting *Who Is Bella Pemberton?* and *Aurora's Best-Kept Secret.* She tried to ignore them all and focused on what was good—including the very personal benefit of wearing lighter clothing and having her hair up, so she wasn't unbearably warm all the time. At the office she stayed with short-sleeved dresses and blouses with pencil skirts, sometimes taming her hair into a low ponytail or chignon.

And when the weekend came and she was utterly shattered by her work schedule, she headed to Provence and the château for a few days of rest and unplugging. She'd never worked so hard… or been so invigorated.

Summer was hot in Provence, and now, in early August, the lavender was in bloom. She'd left work early to catch the train to Aix-en-Provence, and was picked up by a car service for the journey to the house. They drove through the countryside in a sea of purply blue, and the tension seeped out of her the closer she got to the château. It was already nearly nine, and she was ready for a glass of wine and perhaps some time looking at the stars. She'd be alone this weekend. Maman had gone back to London for a checkup with Dr. Mallick, and Bella was ready to enjoy the peace and quiet.

Kitchen staff had prepared a light supper for her, and so she first ventured to the wine cellar and then the kitchen, sipping and munching to quell her hunger and thirst. Then she poured a second glass of the very nice chenin blanc that she'd picked and headed to the garden. It was dark now, and the stars peeked out in the blanket of black sky. The nearby lavender fields perfumed the air, and she could pick up notes of thyme, rosemary, tarragon from the herb pots nearby. There was a rich sweetness, too, which made her believe the nectarines and apples in the grove were ripe for picking.

She settled into one of the loungers, tipped it back a bit more, and gazed up at the constellations.

She hadn't been able to forget Charlotte's words about her stepping into the main office. Maman still hadn't said anything about a return date, but she hadn't not said anything, either. It was all up in the air.

It was a punishing pace, but Bella was still learning so of course there was a lot of adjustment. She also had the ability to reconfigure some duties and responsibilities, if need be. Taking time like this—to decompress, to be quiet—was crucial.

When the wine was gone and she'd watched a satellite arc across the night sky, she got up and went inside. She ran a bath with relaxing salts, and then crawled into her bed, sighing with pleasure as the soft sheets encompassed her body.

Her heart ached a little at being alone, but it was okay. Maybe this…maybe it was enough.

Maybe.

Burke had only been to the Pemberton château once in his life, back in his university days, when he'd gone for a bank holiday weekend with William. Late Saturday morning he skipped the last session at his conference in Avignon, rented a car, and made the forty-five-minute drive to see Bella.

It had been quite by chance that he'd known Bella was even there. He'd been talking to William, trying to convince him to pop down for a day or two, and William had said Bella was planning on spending the weekend and that he didn't want to interrupt her as she had been putting in long hours. He'd also mentioned enjoying wedded bliss and seemed reluctant to leave his wife. Burke had laughed; Will was just back from his honeymoon, of course. But the information that

Bella was at the château had made her stick in his thoughts, all through the past two and a half days of meetings, lectures and workshops.

The gates to the château were open and he drove through, his guts churning. He had no idea how she'd react to his arrival. With pleasure? He hoped so. With annoyance, at interrupting her peace? Maybe. He wasn't even sure what he expected from her, what he wanted. But he wanted to see her. The whole "move on" thing wasn't working so well.

At just past noon, the heat was starting to climb. The forecast predicted a hot one today, peaking at ninety degrees. He knocked on the door and waited, then knocked again. What if she'd gone out? He should have called first. Should have—

His thoughts were cut off by the opening of the door by a young woman in plain black trousers and a white tailored shirt.

He took out his French, which was rusty though he'd gotten in some practice during the conference. "Bonjour. Arabella *est ici*?"

"*Oui, monsieur. Un instant, s'il vous plaît.*"

She was here. Thank God. The maid ushered him inside and he waited in the foyer. The house was just as grand as he remembered, with high, soaring ceilings and beautiful finish work. The manor house was beautiful, but this…the château was stunning.

And then Bella was walking toward him, a slightly confused smile on her face. "Burke? What are you doing here?"

"I was at a conference in Avignon. Will said you were here, and I thought…well, I thought I'd drop by."

It was nearly an hour from his hotel to her château. Not exactly in the neighborhood. He felt like a fool.

Worse, he felt like the situation was totally out of his control. He'd been the one to say he didn't want a relationship, and at the first opportunity, here he was. He understood her being confused. *He* was confused.

When he looked at her, though, it seemed as if everything from the last three weeks clicked into place. All the anxiety, all the edginess, all the questioning, just fell away. It felt as if this was exactly where he was meant to be.

And that was scary as hell.

She was looking at him curiously. "Drop by?"

He nodded. Where had his cool charm gone? His control in every situation? Maybe this was a huge mistake.

"I hope it's all right. If it's not, I can leave."

There was a moment of hesitation. He couldn't tell by her expression what she was feeling. Her face looked exactly like it had when they'd first encountered each other in Italy—guarded.

But then her tense facial muscles relaxed and

her eyes warmed the slightest bit. "It's okay. To be honest, it's good to see you."

"I've missed you," he admitted.

She looked around, as if suddenly realizing they were still in the foyer. "We don't need to stand here all day," she said. "Let's go to the garden. There's nice shade."

He followed her through, with no time to gawk at the open doors and the opulent rooms beyond. Bella's hips swayed gently as she walked, her posture straight and elegant. Her hair was up, too, and her small collar only partially concealed the scar there. There were so many things he wanted to ask her, but they could wait. Right now he wanted to take the temperature of the situation. Get his emotional feet beneath him.

The garden was a wonder. Stone steps, myriad planters of fragrant herbs and flowers, and Aleppo pines created an oasis of relaxation. "Wow. I'd forgotten how beautiful this is."

"Do you want to walk? There are some great views from the grove."

"If you like."

She continued on, leading him outside the garden to the lemon and nectarine grove on the property. The trees provided slight shade from the sun, and the scent of the ripening fruit was nothing short of delicious. But it was Bella he was entranced with. There was a confidence in her now that hadn't been there even a month ago.

She was stronger. Tougher. Happier? He wondered. Because he'd been mostly miserable since she'd turned his life upside down.

They crested the knoll in the grove and Burke caught his breath. Fields of lavender waved below them, a carpet of purple against the robin's-egg blue of the sky. "Wow," he breathed, taking a deep breath of the perfumed air. "I can understand why you came for a weekend. It's peace and quiet and aromatherapy all in one."

She finally smiled, and his heart gave a little bump.

"It's been a month of changes," she admitted. "First the wedding, and Maman being ill, and us, and filling in for her, and then the big reveal." She looked up at him with a sheepish smile and shrugged. "For someone used to being in the background, I really outdid myself. I didn't realize until I got here last night what a toll it's taken."

That admission concerned him. "You have to be careful not to burn yourself out."

"The work is fine. Hard, but fine. Emotionally…different story."

"I'm sorry if I contributed to that."

She was looking over the lavender field again. "Not contributed, exactly. More like…the catalyst. It needed to happen. I'm glad it happened, and I have no regrets. But it's been a lot."

He wanted to touch her and knew he didn't

have the right. "I have regrets. One of them being how I treated you in London."

She turned to face him again but said nothing. Waiting for him to elaborate, he supposed.

"Can we…maybe sit on that bench over there?" He gestured at an old stone bench at the edge of the grove, overlooking the valley below. It looked exactly like a place where lovers would go for a rendezvous or someone would visit to be alone with their thoughts. Made for intimacy, he realized. And while that scared him, he knew he'd bungled his earlier conversations with her and needed to make her understand better.

"Sure, if you want."

The bench was warm from the sun. She sat and then he sat after, and then, on impulse, reached over to take her hand.

"Bella, that night after we…" His throat caught and he cleared it. "After we made love, I told you I had to be honest with you about what I wanted. That I was focused on my career. That was true… but what I didn't say, what I should have said, was that I care about you. That you matter. That walking away from you was going to be the hardest thing I'd ever done. If I made you feel…disposable, I'm so very sorry."

He cringed as he said the word *disposable*.

She sighed. "I'm not going to lie. It stung that you found it so easy, after everything I'd shared with you."

"It wasn't as easy as you think." A million thoughts raced through his head, ones that he didn't want to face or deal with right now. "I know I seemed like I had it all together. I fooled myself into thinking that no one would get hurt or it would be no big deal."

"So you kissed me on the plane."

"And in the elevator. And a lot of other places."

Places being both geographical and intimate. Awareness buzzed between them again, like a bee searching for nectar in the garden blossoms. He could feel it, the longing, the need. Being with her now made him reconsider everything he thought was true.

She leaned back and tipped her face to the sun, closing her eyes. "Last night I wished you were here, and now you are. And now I don't know what to do about it. Nothing has changed."

"No, nothing has changed," he murmured, and he slid closer and leaned over to touch his lips to the corner of her mouth.

Her breath fluttered out, a delicate release that fueled his desire even further. What if they could make it work? What if they didn't give up quite yet? He didn't know how, but in this particular moment it didn't seem to matter. What mattered was he was here with her again and everything that had been wrong for the past weeks was suddenly right again.

He shifted, deepened the kiss just a little, keeping it soft and tentative but removing the question that had been unspoken in the first kiss. She responded by lifting a hand and curving it gently around his neck, a subtle pressure holding him in place, close to her.

He nibbled on her lower lip, made himself break the contact. "Bella. I can't seem to shake you and I don't know what to do about it."

"Me either. But I want this. I wanted it the first time and I haven't yet had my fill. I know where things stand with you. I respect that. But you're here and…"

"Shh…" He put his finger over her lips. "Yes. And as much as making love to you in the lemon grove would be hot as hell, I want to be able to take my time. Not be some hurried thing in the grass."

"Then we should go back to the château."

"You're sure?"

"Very sure. I never wanted you to walk away in the first place." She put her hand on his face. "Burke, I've waited so long to start living. If I can't have you forever, let me at least have what you can give me now. With no promises and no regrets."

It should have been music to his ears, but instead it sent a rush of remorse through his heart. "You deserve better," he whispered.

"Let me decide what I deserve."

There was no arguing with her. She was as

stubborn as they came and it was foolish to dis-
agree when he wanted the exact same thing she
did. He got up from the bench and held out his
hand, and she took it.

Then they raced through the grove to the gardens and into the house.

# CHAPTER THIRTEEN

BELLA WAS NEARLY breathless when she reached her room on the third floor of the château. She and Burke had dashed through the heat of the afternoon to get to the house, then up the stairs. He'd stopped her twice to steal panty-melting kisses, and only the thought of an errant staff member popping around a corner kept Bella from hauling him down on top of her right then and there.

She opened the door to her room, pulled him inside by the hand and shut the door. Firmly.

In the space of a heartbeat he had her pressed against the hard wood of the door. The first night had been gentle and tender, and careful. *Careful* was not a word to describe the fire running through her veins now, or the way Burke kissed his way from collarbone to navel as he undid her blouse with rough fingers and dropped it to the floor.

It was a hurried dash to rid themselves of the

rest of their clothes and then they were naked on her bed, touching and tasting and desperate to get closer, closer.

Burke got up for a moment and went for his jeans, grabbing a condom from the front pocket. "Sure of yourself, were you?" She rose up on her elbows, her hair cascading down her back as she watched him tear open the package. God, he was beautiful, all dark hair and smooth skin and strength.

"Not at all, but if there was a remote chance this was going to happen, I wasn't going to get caught without protection."

"I admire your foresight."

He got back on the bed with her and looped an arm around her hips, pulling her down several inches. "I hope in a moment you'll admire something else."

She let out a cry of delight.

This was different. So different and free and equal and oh-so-satisfying. It was need and want and giving and taking all at once. Her skin grew slick with sweat in the afternoon heat. Burke, too, had a sheen of sweat on his shoulders and she leaned forward to lick at it. He didn't hold back this time, and she lost herself in it. Their first time had been perfect, but this time it was primal and she loved it even more. Loved knowing she had the power to make Burke lose control.

* * *

When they finally slid, boneless, back onto the covers, panting with exertion and glowing with perspiration, Bella started to laugh. It rose up from her belly to her chest, up her throat and out her mouth in a rich, replete sound that was disbelief and satisfaction wrapped up in one.

She couldn't move and couldn't care less.

Burke swore lightly, and she laughed.

"Thank you," she said, her voice deliberately soft.

"For what?" he asked.

"For losing control a little bit. For being a little wild and less restrained and…calculated. I don't mean that the way it sounds," she amended. "It was just the first time you seemed focused on doing things step by step, I guess. This time…it was like you couldn't help yourself."

"I could have if you'd asked. But I'm awfully glad you didn't."

"Oh, me, too."

Finally she rolled over to face him. She no longer worried about him seeing the scars on her arms and shoulders, and it was lovely to know she could be this way—totally naked with him— and his gaze wasn't going to drop in shock or dismay or disgust.

"I think we need to talk about the fact that we can't seem to keep our hands off each other. I mean, we went from barely talking to in my bed in less than thirty minutes."

"I'm sorry. I didn't intend—"

She cut him off. "It wasn't a complaint. But we can't keep doing this, Burke. Desperate to be together in one way and pushing each other away in another. Nothing has changed. At least nothing that I can see."

The shadowed look came into his eyes again, and he started to move away but she grabbed his arm and kept him on the bed. "No, don't run away. I know there's more you're not saying. I wish you'd be honest with me."

When he was quiet, she let out a huff of frustration. "I shared so much with you. It hurts me that you don't trust me with the same. This has to do with more than just your job, doesn't it?"

This time when he went to get up, she let him, and he reached for his boxers and pulled them on. She understood the action more than he might think. He was feeling naked, both physically and emotionally. Even underwear added to a sense of protection.

She, on the other hand, made no move to get dressed. She had nothing to hide. Not now.

He sat on the edge of the bed and rested his elbows on his knees. Bella scooted over a bit, wondering what could possibly be bothering him. "Hey," she said softly. "If there's something you need to talk about, I hope you know by now that you're safe with me."

He turned his head and met her eyes. "I know that. Honestly, Bella, I don't know what I'm doing. I've had such a clear path until a few weeks ago. I knew what I wanted and I didn't stray from that trajectory. And then you came along and everything changed. And yeah, it was from the moment we slept together. Not because of you, but because of me. Because…" He hesitated and took a shuddering breath. "Because my mind and heart are at complete odds. What I feel for you is something I never really wanted to feel for anyone, and it comes down to my parents, really."

Nothing he might have said surprised her more. "You told me it was because of your career."

"It was. It is! But deep down it's more than that. My career—I love it, but I've used it, too, as an excuse to keep myself distanced from people. Damn. This is hard."

"Most conversations of this type are," she agreed.

She slid over and wrapped her arms around him. "Burke, you helped me so much. You were right from the start—I had to start talking about the accident, facing what had happened and not hiding away. Being with you was like someone lit a candle inside me. I stopped being so afraid.

I feel…liberated. If I can help you in some way, with whatever you're struggling with, I want to. Because I know it's something. I can see it behind your eyes."

He sighed. "It is something."

She waited, because she sensed he needed her to be patient.

"When I was a kid, I thought our life was pretty happy. I mean, my father was gone a lot. I thought he was so important. The viscount, you know? And he had business. All of his business interests—and he'd invested in a lot of different schemes—got his attention. Mum always seemed happy and there was me and my sisters, and we did stuff together. It was, I thought, a good childhood."

She sensed a "but" coming and held her tongue.

"But when I was sixteen, and away at school, I went to a friend's for a long weekend. We went into a pub for food and I saw my father in there with a woman. Before you say anything, I didn't misinterpret what I saw. It was plainly obvious. He wasn't even trying to hide it."

Burke turned his head and looked at her. "My dad, my hero, was having an affair. And everything I'd known as stable and secure was now tainted."

Her heart melted for the boy he'd been. Her own parents had been so devoted to each other.

She would have been crushed if she'd discovered they'd ever been unfaithful. "Oh, Burke, I'm so sorry."

"I know. I'm thirty and should be over it. But I watched my dad for years, wondering with each trip he went on if he were really going on business or if he was seeing her. Or worse, someone else. Wondering if my mother knew, and how long it had been that way. I somehow think she must have, but she put on such a happy face. Everything was a lie. I never, ever want to hurt someone like that, Bella."

"But you wouldn't. You're not your father."

"No? I've buried myself at work so that I don't have to have any relationships of consequence. And the one time I do find someone who makes me care, shows me what it might be like, I send her away. Because I'm afraid of hurting her. And worse—because I'm afraid of my own feelings."

She kissed his shoulder. "You don't want to become him. I get it. But I think there's more. Burke, it's clear to me that this hurt you very deeply. If you keep your relationships 'on the surface' and without any real depth, then no one else can hurt *you* like he did, either."

His back shuddered as he took in a breath. "I don't know how to love you, Bella. I never learned. But maybe it's time. If you can share your scars with the world, maybe I can share mine with you. But it's a scary thing, giving someone else this much of myself. You need to know that."

She hadn't expected something like this. What she remembered of his father, the previous Viscount Downham, was a handsome, charismatic man who looked like an older version of Burke, with crinkly brown eyes and a warm smile. He'd been charming. And he'd been friends with her father, too. "Your dad was well-liked. That must have been hard for you, knowing his flaws."

He nodded. "Especially in the earlier years. He could charm all my friends, and I wanted to shout at them, 'You don't know!' Ugh. It's been hard the last few weeks. I've tried all my life to not be like him, and it turns out I'm more like him than I thought."

She moved to sit beside him, tucking her ankle beneath her so she was facing his profile. "Nonsense. What you did is nothing like a man cheating on his wife. You were trying to protect yourself, and I think protect me as well. From being hurt. But what hurt was being without you."

"Bella. You don't know what you're saying."

"I do. I know how I feel right now. I feel honored that you shared this with me. I feel amazed and beautiful, knowing you couldn't wait to take me to bed. I feel like the moment you hugged me beside the Baresis' pool, something inside me started to heal. You did that, Burke. You did."

He swallowed tightly. "I don't know what to do next."

"Nor do I. But come back to bed and hold me, and at some point it'll become clear for us. I can't believe that this is the end, not after everything we've shared. Let's just be for a while. Whenever we have a pressing problem at work, Maman always says to let it rest for a while and the answer will come. So let's be patient and see what happens."

He reached out and pulled her close. "You are one in a million, Arabella Pemberton. It's no wonder I love you."

The words hit her like a jolt to the chest, an explosion of fireworks that sent sparks outward until she was filled with light, body and soul. "You love me?"

He nodded, his eyes solemn. "I do. I don't know what comes next, but if I'm determined to be honest, you should know how I feel. It's too big a gift to keep to myself."

She bit down on her lip to keep from crying, and then Burke snuggled her in his arms as they nestled beneath the sheets of her bed. It was midafternoon and she didn't care. There was nowhere else in the entire world she would rather be. He loved her and she loved him. Surely there was some way they could work out a way to be together.

* * *

Burke slid out of bed a few hours later, refreshed from his postcoital nap. He was trying to think of possibilities. Ways to make their relationship work. Maybe they didn't have to rush any big decisions. Maybe they could do the long-distance thing for a little while. After all, London to Paris was easily navigated and they both had the means. Besides, Bella would only be filling in for Aurora for a little while longer, and then surely her schedule would become slightly more flexible.

He was feeling optimistic and lighter than he had in ages as he slipped into his jeans and shirt. He wanted to let her sleep; William had said she'd been putting in a ton of hours and she looked so peaceful, so beautiful beneath the pale sheet, her soft skin glowing and her lips full and slightly opened as she breathed deeply. He'd just go downstairs and maybe sit in the garden again, get some relaxation himself.

He was just crossing the cobblestones toward the grouping of chairs when his phone vibrated in his pocket, signaling a text message. He ignored it. There wasn't anything so important he needed to answer right now. But when his ringtone sounded a few moments later, he frowned and took it out, swiping the lock screen.

Will's number popped up.

"Hey, what's up?" he asked, pressing the phone to his ear.

"Go check the link I just sent you. I'm sorry, Burke. Hate being the bearer of bad news."

Dread settled in Burke's gut as he looked down at the phone and swiped over to his direct messages. Will had sent him a link to an online story from a well-known news outlet. The dread intensified, making his blood run cold.

He scanned the first three paragraphs, and there it was, his name. The story of how the accident had caused Bella's disfigurement and that he and Bella had been in the car with Royce. The credibility of the source could not be disputed: it was Fiona, the girl he'd taken along with him, and only contacted once since—the day after the accident, asking if she was okay.

She hadn't wanted her name in the news, either. She'd looked older but he'd later discovered she was only fifteen. All of them drinking underage. It had suited them all to have their names left out as minors.

Until now. Because tabloids paid good money to sources.

He thought he was going to be sick to his stomach.

He sank into a chair, cold despite the bright sun shining down on him. He put the phone back to his ear. "Dammit, Will."

"I know. Though I suppose once Bella stopped hiding, it was bound to come out."

"Has Charlotte seen it yet?"

"I sent it to her first, and told her I was calling you. If I know Charlotte, she's going to come up with a plan for damage control and present it as a fait accompli before calling Bella. Where are you?"

Burke put his forehead in his hand. "I'm at the château. Bella's inside." Sleeping. After making love to him. Dammit all.

"You went to see her."

"We have stuff to work out." He didn't say more than that. He wasn't the kind to bring other people into his personal life, although Will was his best friend. But Will was also Bella's brother. "We care about each other a lot, Will. But it's not simple."

There was a pause. Then Will spoke, his voice firm in Burke's ear. "It's never simple. But you're the best man I know, Burke. I could see this coming in Italy and thought it might be something wonderful. That being said, if you hurt my sister, I'm going to have to mess you up a bit."

Burke choked out a laugh. He was still reeling from being called a good man. Will might not say so if he knew Burke's thoughts right now. News like this—about a drunk driving accident being hidden away—could affect his professional life.

He was so close to getting a dream job. What if this messed it up?

"Will, I need to go. But I appreciate the heads-up."

"Phone if you need anything."

They hung up and Burke let out a deep sigh.

Just when things started to come together. Why did life always have to be so…complicated?

# CHAPTER FOURTEEN

BELLA WOKE ALONE and looked around her. Burke was gone, and for a moment she had a flash of fear that it hadn't been real, or that he'd dressed and left her, gone back to Avignon or London or…

But then she let out her breath and told herself that was ridiculous. Burke would not run out on her like that. He wasn't that kind of man. So she slipped out of bed, put on a cool sundress, and went searching.

She found him in the garden, sitting with his head in his hands. Worry spiraled through her. Something was wrong. Something more than deep thought. Was he regretting what he'd told her? Being with her? She desperately hoped not, but she'd face this head-on. She was used to it by now.

"Hi," she said softly.

He lifted his head. His eyes were shadowed with tension and his lips were set. "Hi. Sorry. I woke up and needed some air."

He was having second thoughts, wasn't he?

"What's going on?"

He held out his phone. "Call your sister."

She froze, hand outstretched. "Oh God. Is it Maman?"

"No! No. I'm so sorry. I never even thought of that. No, your mother is fine. But you need to call Charlotte. Then we can talk."

This was not helping to dispel her fears. She punched in Charlotte's number and wasn't even greeted with a hello. "Burke. I take it you've heard?"

"It's Bella on Burke's phone. What's going on? He hasn't told me anything."

There was a big sigh, and then Charlotte cleared her throat. "Fiona came forward with the story of the crash. It's all over the media now. I'm guessing she got a good payout for all the details."

Bella closed her eyes. They'd hoped this wouldn't happen, but it had always been a possibility. "She named names?"

"Yes. Burke's and yours. Royce was already a matter of record. He wasn't a minor."

"So what do we do?"

"You do nothing for now. You stay at the château. In an hour or so I'll send over a document with talking points we can use to respond, but I don't think this is worth an actual Aurora press release. We're also getting interview requests. I've denied them all."

"Thank you, Charlotte. I'd like for us to not be reactionary and to take a measured response to this. Basically, not overreact in general."

"Exactly. Thank you for that, because I didn't want to have to talk you down from a panic attack or anything."

"I don't have panic attacks."

Charlotte laughed. "True. But you've been through a lot the past few weeks. Thanks for being so consistent."

"That's me." Sometimes she wished she weren't. There was a certain strain around the pressure to remain levelheaded and consistent. Not that she'd have it any other way, but it was there just the same.

She looked over at Burke. He was clearly not taking this well. "Listen, I'll look for your email later. I'm going to go for now. Is that okay?"

"Of course. I'll be in touch soon."

"Thank you, Charlotte."

They hung up and Bella handed the phone back to Burke. "Well, I guess the cat's out of the bag. I rather hoped it wouldn't be."

"Me, too." He ran his hand through his hair. "I just had my meeting at the Royal Brompton. Everything was looking so good there. Now my face is going to be on some stupid magazine."

Bella sat down beside him. "My father used

to call them 'scurrilous rags,'" she said, offering a small smile. "The story won't last forever, Burke. You were seventeen. And you weren't driving."

He stared at her. "At dinner, that night in London, I told you what my biggest fear was. You knew. Don't make me feel as if I shouldn't be upset, Bella. That's not fair."

She kept a lid on her own bubbling feelings. "Of course you're allowed to be upset. I'm just trying to make you see that the fallout won't be that bad." She put her hand over his. "Darling, if people didn't survive gossip and tattling, no one would ever stay in business." She had a sudden idea. "Listen, why don't you talk to Charlotte? She's used to running damage control. I know she'd walk you through some of this as well and put your mind at ease."

He stood up suddenly. "You expected this."

She frowned. "I always knew it was a possibility. Fiona was the one wild card we couldn't control."

"And yet you knew how I felt and you went ahead anyway." He turned away, paced a few steps, and turned back. "Wow."

An hour ago they'd been professing their love and now this. She wasn't prepared for this roller coaster of emotion and wanted off. "First of all, I didn't need to show my scars for Fiona to come forward. The Pembertons are high-profile enough that she could have come forward at any time and it would have been a story. And secondly, you were the one who pushed me away in London, saying we didn't have a relationship. So what, I'm supposed to hide who I am forever? Do you realize what you're saying?"

Her heart slammed in her chest as adrenaline kicked in from the anxiety and emotion running through her veins.

"No, of course not." He swore. "There are no winners in this."

"Clearly," she answered.

He stared at her for several moments, and she held his gaze, unwilling to back down.

"I wish I'd never gotten in that car that night," he finally said, his voice hoarse.

"Me, too, but I did, and you did, and a boy died, and we were all hurt. At some point you have to accept it and move on. Feeling guilty solves nothing. Hiding what it did to you—that solves nothing. I faced my biggest fear and nothing dire happened. I'm still here and alive. Maybe it's time you faced yours, too."

"But you didn't have the right to choose that for me, and now I have no choice."

He wasn't wrong. And he wasn't right, either. She softened her voice. "Burke, my choice to be open about myself has caused you pain. If I'd chosen to not be open, I would have spared you pain but harmed myself. You walked away from me. I was hurt. I was not angry. Nothing I did was out of maliciousness or trying to hurt you. Instead, it was about choosing me, for the first time in forever." She pressed her fist to her heart. "But I'm truly sorry that this has hurt you. I am. Like you said—no winners."

"You've won."

His sharp words were a knife to the heart. "Have I? An hour ago you said you loved me. Now it looks as though this changes everything. I'm not really feeling like a winner right now."

His face changed, dropped into a mask of sadness. "Bella."

"Maybe this is just too messy. I'm sorry, Burke, I can't deal with any more right now."

He nodded. "I'll go. I need to go back to London and see what's to be done, anyway. I'm sure this has gotten back to Mum as well. You're right. It's messy as hell."

Perhaps he was misunderstanding. She hadn't meant in general, she'd meant for them as a couple...or not as a couple. But as he left her there on the patio, she realized that twice now he'd put her aside to protect himself. The compromise she'd longed to work for with him was gone.

And with it, her hope for her future.

Her mother had been very lucky. She'd had the company and a husband who loved and doted on her. Maybe Bella just needed to be content with the professional success. It just cut cruelly to get a taste of love only to have it snatched away… again.

Burke waited two days after arriving in London to go see his mother. In that time, the story had made the rounds in the weekly tabloids, websites and entertainment programs on TV. Arabella was a big draw. Throw in a viscount and the gossip was that much spicier.

He'd gone back to work yesterday to whispers, which he'd ignored. Long looks of speculation which he also ignored. But he found himself snappish, which wasn't his usual style, either with coworkers or with patients. He had yet to hear from the Royal Brompton, but at this point everyone had to be aware of the scandal.

His mother still lived in the family home, a lovely dwelling in Kensington with ten bedrooms and seven baths and a surprisingly peaceful garden where she had taken up growing her own herbs and lettuces. When Burke walked in that Tuesday morning, a measure of calm came over him.

They met in the breakfast room, a sunny, welcoming space that had windows overlooking the garden. Beyond that, leafy trees provided more privacy as the property backed onto Holland Park. "Burke, darling. It's so good to see you. I've put out coffee. Have you eaten?"

He hadn't. His appetite was off, had been since leaving France. "I'm fine, Mum. Coffee is great."

"I'll send down for some cake. I know for a fact there's a fresh lemon drizzle waiting to be cut into."

Mothers. They reverted to making sure you ate enough in times of strife. He smiled a little. "Cake would be lovely."

She came forward, looked up into his face and then stood on tiptoe to give him a hug. "It's going to be all right, you know," she murmured, patting his back. "You just have to weather the storm."

Her choice of words made him wonder. Within a few minutes they were seated at the table, both with cups of hot coffee and slices of still-warm cake before them.

He drank. She drank. Then she put her cup down and looked at him evenly. "What is it you want to ask me? I can tell there's something. You might as well get it out."

Everything inside him cramped. He wasn't sure how to do this, but he did know that his life, for the first time since the accident, felt as if it were in utter shambles. "I've messed something up, and I don't know how to fix it."

Isabel waved a hand. "If it's about the accident, this will blow over in a few days. Another story will take its place."

"It's partly about that. But it's…bigger," he said, struggling to find the right words. "You see, Mum, I've gone and fallen in love with Bella Pemberton."

Isabel put down her fork, the cake still speared on the tines. "Oh. I see."

"Do you?"

"She made the news with her scars. I wondered if they were from the accident."

"They are. She's so beautiful and brave and strong. And I've messed up everything by just trying to do the right thing." He met her gaze. "My whole life I've tried to do the right thing and it hasn't always worked out so well."

Quiet fell between them for a few moments. Then he screwed up his courage and prepared to break his mother's heart.

"Dad had an affair when I was sixteen."

Isabel took a long, slow inhale, then released it. "I know."

His mouth dropped open. "You knew?"

"It wasn't his first." Sadness colored her hazel eyes. "I had you and the girls. Our marriage... I probably shouldn't have stayed. Not after the first infidelity. I agreed to stay and raise you three here, and he promised to be discreet."

"It was in the middle of a very public pub. He was there with...her."

"Did he know you saw him?"

"No, never."

"I see. And this has to do with Bella because?"

Isabel picked up her coffee now and took a

long drink. Burke was so surprised by her question that he sat back, considering. "Because she deserves better than what you got. She deserves someone to dote on her, to not be married to his job. Which I am."

"Why?"

"I'm sorry?"

She let out a frustrated sigh. "Why are you married to your job?"

"The hours are heinous."

"No, not good enough." She folded her hands in her lap. "Fill in the blank. 'If I'm married to my job, then I'm not…'"

She let the end of the sentence hang. *…not married to a person, and I can't hurt them.*

"Go ahead and say it, Burke. It's all right." Her voice was soft, gentle. Understanding, even.

"I would never want to hurt her the way that Father hurt you," Burke admitted. "He was never here. He was always gone for work. Then when he was gone, he was with other women. You deserved better, Mum. And so does Bella. And the truth is, I do love my job. I'm dedicated to it. I've been sick to my stomach for three days wondering what's happening with the opportunity at the Royal Brompton. I'm so selfish."

He pushed away his coffee in disgust.

"Oh, what a bunch of codswallop."

He lifted his head. His mother's mouth was

set in a firm line and she was frowning at him. "What is?"

"The selfish part. You don't have a selfish bone in your body. So what if you're worried about your career? You've spent years building it. The last thing you want is for something far in your past to come up and ruin it."

"Thank you!" he said, relieved she understood.

"That doesn't mean I think you're right. It just means I understand why you might feel that way. Do you know what I think?"

"Do I have a choice?" he grumbled.

"You came here, darling," she reminded him. She wasn't wrong.

"I think you're using your career to run away. You're afraid. Not of your reputation. You're afraid of yourself. You've carried this secret around for too long and you're wondering if you're like your father. After all, if you could make such a poor decision the night of the party, who's to say you won't be that irresponsible later?"

He pushed away from the table, turning his back on her and walking to the window. She'd punched right through all his barriers, even the ones he hadn't realized he'd constructed. He hadn't been able to hate his father because he'd been too busy hating himself for getting in the car. For not taking the keys from Royce. For all of it.

She got up and followed him, and he didn't look down but felt the pressure of her hand on his arm.

"Burke, you are not your father. Just because you carry the same title doesn't mean you'll make the same mistakes. Just because you share the same DNA doesn't mean you're predestined to walk in his footsteps."

Tears pricked behind his eyes, burning hot. "I can't stand the idea of disappointing people."

"I know. I've watched you wrap yourself in charm and charisma and even compassion for over a decade, all to protect yourself. If Bella Pemberton has broken through that wall, then more power to her. It's about time you fell on your ass in love. Your sisters and I were starting to think it wouldn't happen."

Bella. Just the thought of her made his heart ache. "How did you do it, Mum? How did you stay here and pretend to be so happy when you had to be dying inside?" He turned his head to look down at her.

"I made my own choices, Burke. And I had you and the girls, and we had a good life. There were fun times. And I didn't hate your father. He was, in many ways, a good man. But we didn't share a deep passion. That's what I regret. I didn't love him, so how can I hate him for searching for it somewhere else?"

Burke shook his head. "Don't blame yourself for him cheating."

"He made his choices. But I also made mine. My wish for my children has always been for them to find someone they love, truly love right to the depths of their being. Is that Bella for you?"

He thought of her and her soft smile, wide eyes, strong chin. The way she made him laugh and how she felt in his arms. "I think it might be."

"And you're standing here in my breakfast room, worrying about some job so you don't have to think about all the ways you can screw this up. You're a smart man, Burke, and a talented physician. But you're being a coward."

A lump formed in his throat. "I came here for some love and support."

"My love and support comes in the form of kicking your ass."

He chuckled. This was not what he'd expected at all. First, that she knew about his father's affairs, and second, that she'd give his head a good shake instead of giving him a loving hug.

Isabel's voice gentled. "Burke, all I can say is this. Jobs and opportunities come and go. But when you find the one person who makes everything make sense, you have to latch onto that and never let it go."

He thought of his potential job, and how he'd

been so afraid the truth would ruin his chances. And then he thought of Bella, touching his shoulder as he told her his deepest secret, and knew he'd already blown his biggest chance at happiness. She'd forgiven him once, but there was no guarantee she'd forgive him another time. "I think I might have messed it up for good," he murmured, his heart sore.

"Then you have to figure out what you're willing to do to get her back. And then tell her. Show her."

He looked at his mother. There were tears on her cheeks, and he put his arm around her and tucked her close. "I'm sorry, Mum. More sorry than you can know."

"Don't be. Besides, I'm only fifty-four. There's still time for a second chance for me, you know."

He smiled at that, gave her arm a squeeze. "I'm going to have to make some changes," he said, but oddly enough, the idea wasn't quite as terrifying as it had been less than an hour ago. Now what was scary was not knowing if Bella would say yes.

"Eat your cake first," she said, moving away from his embrace. "And have more coffee. I've missed you. Maybe we can talk through it together, hmm?"

As Burke returned to the table, a new calm settled over him. The one thing he had to do was make things right with Bella. If he could do that, everything else would fall into place. The only thing worse than being afraid of failure was the regret to be found in not trying.

And, damn, he was tired of regret.

# CHAPTER FIFTEEN

IT TOOK NEARLY two more weeks for Burke to head to Paris. In that time he'd met with his current boss, had a meeting with the directors at the Royal Brompton, and come to Paris two days ago for more meetings. He was currently sitting on the balcony of his vacation rental overlooking the river and drinking a very strong coffee.

Today he needed to see Arabella, and he was scared to death. There was a very good chance that she was going to take one look at him and send him on his way. After all, he'd turned away from her twice now because of his own fears. She deserved so much better.

He'd been tested and he'd come up short. He didn't like that about himself at all. He just hoped it wasn't too late to fix, because he did love her. And if he could get out of his own way, they might just have a chance at some happiness.

He checked his phone for the time and noted it was nearly nine. It would take him twenty minutes or so to make his way to the Aurora Inc. offices and hope she wasn't in a meeting. Was it a mistake to go see her at work? He was afraid that if he asked her to meet with him, she'd say no. But what if she refused to see him at all? They hadn't spoken since he'd walked away from her at the château.

So he went inside, locked the door to the balcony, put his dirty cup in the sink, and went to the bathroom to brush his teeth and give himself a final once-over. His stomach was in knots, but he made sure he had his phone and his wallet and went out the door to hail a taxi.

He'd never been inside the Aurora Inc. building before. It was a gorgeous place, with marble floors and a reception area that had white-veined marble counters and "Aurora" in stylized lettering behind the desks. The admin staff were dressed in all black and white as well. It was classy as heck.

"Good morning. I'm here to see Arabella Pemberton."

"Do you have an appointment, sir?"

"No, I'm afraid I do not."

"Your name?"

"Burke Phillips."

"Let me call up to her assistant and see if she has time in her schedule today."

Of course there would be gatekeepers. Bella was effectively running the company. Just last week Aurora had surprised everyone with the announcement that she was stepping back from many of her duties and that the board of directors had approved Bella as her successor. He was hugely proud and somewhat intimidated.

"Sir? Ms. Pemberton is currently in a meeting, but her assistant says she can meet with you in forty minutes. Take the elevator to the fourth floor and give your name to the main reception." She gestured toward the elevator bank to his right.

"Thank you," he replied, wondering why his mouth was suddenly dry. Maybe because his whole future depended on how the next hour went?

He took the elevator up and gave his name at the desk, again with white marble and the stylized Aurora lettering, only on a smaller scale. The receptionist led him down a hallway to a small seating area, offered him a coffee and then left him alone to wait. He held on to the black mug, turning it in his hands but not drinking. He was jittery and didn't need another coffee to jack him up further.

He waited thirty minutes. Forty. Forty-five. Fifty. If she was trying to torture him, it was working.

And then she came around the corner, dressed in a white power suit, speaking to another woman in flawless French as she smiled and handed off a portfolio. Finally, finally, she turned to Burke. "Good morning."

"Hi."

He didn't know what else to say. She frowned a little. "Hang on a moment," she said, and disappeared around the corner to her assistant's desk, the woman he'd just seen her with. He heard her speaking, again in French, but couldn't make out quite what she was saying. In seconds she was back. "Come on into my office, where we can talk."

Her office was a huge room, with a stunning desk, chair, credenza, bookcase and art on the walls—all art that shouted Aurora Inc. to him. Gone was the black-and-white signature scheme. The photographic art provided wild bursts of color—dramatic sweeps of fabric in red and orange, a cascade of jewels in rich tones of ruby, sapphire, emerald, topaz. A model's face, dark skin with striking, powerful makeup. The entire collection was a statement of passion and power, and he marveled that it had all come from her, the woman who had barely met his gaze in Italy. He knew without a doubt that these choices were not her mother's. When his girl chose to step into the light, she did it with style. *She owned it.*

"You like these?" she asked, following his gaze.

"I do. You've had them put in? They don't seem like your mother's style."

"I did." She smiled slightly. "I don't want to come in and change everything. Maman was and is a fantastic, smart, dynamic leader. But I want to put my own stamp on things, too. This seemed a good place to start."

He nodded. Looked at her. Felt the air strangling in his throat. "Bella, I wish we could go back to Italy, or that day in London at the butterfly house, and that I could do things right instead of messing it all up."

"But we can't," she answered, and there was a note of sorrow in her voice. "Twice, Burke. Twice you let me hope and believe. And twice you walked away. I'm a strong woman but I wasn't ready for that."

"I know. God, I know." He ran his hand through his hair. They were standing there, in front of her desk, and he wanted to pull her into his arms. He wanted reassurance. Which was stupid because he was the one who should be giving it. "I handled everything wrong."

"We slept together and everything changed. Up to that point you'd been wonderful, open, caring. Perfect. Then it was like you became a stranger. When you left the last time, I realized that I probably don't know who you are. And if I don't know who you are, how can I love you?"

It did sound ominously like the end, and a desperate fear gripped him. "Bella, please. Just listen to what I have to say. Because you're right.

You're so right. I've got to stop hiding and protecting myself and running way. It's the only way I might have a chance with you at all. Will you listen?"

Her throat worked as she looked at him with soft, wounded eyes. "Of course I will."

He took a breath. He could do this. It was Bella. There was no one in the world he trusted more, and he told her so.

"I have never trusted anyone with my father's secret," he began. "And you already knew about the accident. You know more about me than any other human on earth, and that includes my family."

"Your mother doesn't know about your father?"

"I didn't think so, but she always knew. We talked when I went home. We talked about a lot of things."

She smiled a wobbly smile.

"Anyway," he continued, "I've made a habit of never leaving myself open to be vulnerable. Short-term, shallow relationships, burying myself in work, trying to outrun my past mistakes and determined as hell not to carry on my father's cheating legacy. And then there was you, challenging me on both those things. It scared me to death. So what did I do? Retreat. Run away. I was a coward, Bella, and you deserved better.

You deserved a man who would stand beside you and I wasn't there for you. But I want to be now."

She lifted an eyebrow.

"I know. It sounds like something you heard before." Panic started to grip him and he pushed it away.

She took a moment to glance away, then walked over to one of the windows overlooking the city. He could see the view from where he stood. Paris, the city of light. Full of romance and wonder. Boy, he could use a romance miracle right about now.

"Bella," he tried again, "I need you to know what's happened the past two weeks."

"Okay," she answered, turning back from the window. "So tell me."

She wasn't going to make it easy for him, and he loved her all the more for it. Bella lived life on her own terms, every step of the way. She owned her choices, good and bad. It was time he owned his.

"First I panicked. I'm sure you know it didn't take long for the sub-story to hit the news as well. I'm not as scandalous as the Pembertons, but I was Fiona's companion that night and the press went digging. First, I went to see my mother. I talked to my boss at the hospital about it, and then I met with people at the Royal Brompton. Both were supportive. My family, too. They pointed out that I'd taken the horror that was the accident and used it to do something great with my life. It did motivate me to go into medicine, and I love what I do."

"I know you do. And you're good at it. You're good with people, too, and putting them at ease. Those skills don't always go hand in hand."

Her praise gave him hope. "I also realized that my fear of the story being public wasn't really about my professional life. It was about my personal shame. What I wanted from you in Italy was absolution. But even if you'd given it, I hadn't really forgiven myself. If no one else knew, then it was my cross to bear privately. Private shame, not public. I know now that one is not worse than the other."

"It was not your fault, any more than it was mine. I have my own share of shame and guilt, Burke. I've often looked at my scars as penance. Something I've deserved."

"But you've moved past that in such a big and significant way. It's not just about that. They are also marks of your strength and perseverance. Not a single human on the earth hasn't done something they're ashamed of. You stepped into the light while I hid away. You humbled me more than once, Bella. With your trust and with your strength, which I both admire and also don't deserve. But I want to. So much. I want to be worthy of you. I want us to try. I'm here asking you to give me one last chance. I want to become the man I'm meant to be, and I want to do it with you."

Her lip trembled a bit. "That all sounds very pretty. But I'm a bit raw where you're concerned, Burke. I left myself open to you and you turned me away. How do I know you won't do it again?"

He went to her, reached down and gently took one of her hands in his, so glad he'd listened to his mother and had been prepared to show her and not just give her words. "Because I'm ready to prove it. I know you said I'm married to my career, and you're not entirely wrong. It's demanding and I love it. But I don't have to do it in London. There's a position waiting for me here, at St. Joseph's. You need to be here for Aurora. But I do not have to be in London."

She lifted her gaze and her lips dropped open. "You'd move to Paris? But what about the other job? The one that you've been dreaming of?"

He squeezed her fingers. "I could take it and lose you. The truth is, that's not much of a contest. If there's a chance we can make it work, then I want to try. Opportunities come and go. But you...there's only one you, Bella."

She sniffled and blinked rapidly. "Did you practice that?"

He choked on a surprised laugh. "No! I mean, I've been thinking for days what I would say to you, but the moment I saw you everything left my brain."

She pulled her fingers away. "Burke, I didn't do everything right, either."

He stared at her. "What do you mean?"

She took a step back. "I didn't fight for us, either. I knew you were scared but instead of holding your feet to the fire, I walked away. Both at the hospital and at the château. If I'd been willing to fight for us more, we might have worked through things. We might have been able to do this together. But I didn't. Maybe because I had this foolish notion that you had to be perfect. Maybe because, up to that point, you had been perfect. I told myself, and Maman, and Charlotte, that I didn't want to have to beg for affection, but I think maybe the truth was I didn't want to have to work at a relationship. I didn't accept that you could be flawed."

"No," he answered, stepping forward and cupping her face in his hands. "You were a hundred percent right. You did deserve better. So my question is, can we try once more? Because I do love you, Bella. As much as that terrifies me, I do. I'll take the job here and we can put in the work. I want to be the man you deserve so much."

Bella looked into his eyes and saw the man who'd looked back at her at the butterfly house that day, before everything had become so complicated. She understood shame and guilt. She understood trying to outrun the past. What had happened was that she'd been a few steps ahead of him in that regard. Did that mean she should walk away now?

"I want that, too," she murmured, "but I'm scared. I know I seem strong but I'm not sure I could take you bailing when things get complicated again." She had to be honest. It was the only way they had any hope at all.

"Love takes compromise," he finally said. "It took a while for me to realize that. It requires hard work, too. And putting the other person's needs ahead of your own. I wasn't doing that before. Oh, I thought I was being supportive, but only if it didn't affect me. And that was so wrong. I know it's going to take a while to earn that trust back. I don't want us to commute on weekends and weird holidays to build a relationship. I want to be here. By your side. I want to commit to that, Bella. To you."

Bella remembered Charlotte asking her if she would drop everything to move to London for Burke, and her answer had been no. And Charlotte had reminded her that love was a compromise. Charlotte was now based out of London and in return Jacob wasn't going out in the field anymore. They'd both made changes to their lives in order to be together. Burke was making a massive gesture here, willing to turn down a dream opportunity in order to make a relationship with her a priority. It was a huge compromise.

"And what do you expect or need from me?" she asked.

He shook his head. "Don't, Bella. I can't stand it when you make it sound so...transactional. Please, just tell me. Do you love me? Do you think you can love me?"

His voice was thick with emotion and she was shocked to see a sheen of moisture in his eyes. Her heart melted. She remembered all the ways he'd touched her, smiled at her, laughed. She also realized that he'd said the words at the château, but she hadn't said them back. And yet...he was still here.

There were times when she knew she needed to be strong and resolute, and times when she knew she had to be...human. She was great at giving advice but not so great at providing it to herself. So she asked herself what she would say to any of her siblings or friends who came to her in such a situation. And she knew without a doubt that she would say, "Do you love him? If you do, you should give him a chance. Otherwise you will always regret it."

"I do love you," she said softly. Her lip wobbled a bit and she tried to stop it by biting down on it for a moment. "I fell in love with you in London. Not because you were my first but because you treated me with such consideration, such gentleness. You let me be like one of the butterflies at the museum. You let me stay until

I was ready to fly away. Can we have that again, do you think? Because I love that man. And I desperately want to believe that he is the real Burke Phillips."

Burke stepped forward and pulled her into his arms. "God, I've been waiting forever for you to say that." He kissed her cheek, her hair. "I want to be that man again. I want to stop being afraid and living in my father's shadow. Bella, I want to be like you."

"You don't need to be like me. You just have to realize that you are not like your father, and stop blaming yourself for what can't be changed. You're enough, can't you see that?"

He hugged her tighter. "William was right. You give the best advice."

She laughed, and then, as she put her arms around his ribs and held on, the strain and tension and pain of the last few weeks melted away. This was where things were right. In each other's arms.

"Just keep holding me," she whispered. "Everything falls into place when you're holding me."

For long moments they stood there, in a tight embrace.

"I can't hold you like this twenty-four hours a day. We'd never get any work done."

"If you can manage it in the morning and maybe again at night, I think that would be enough."

"You mean that?"

She leaned back and looked into his face. Hope glimmered in his eyes. "Yes, I mean that. Let's try again, Burke. Let's do it right, and not keep anything from each other. Let's help each other through our fears and insecurities. In the end, it'll only make us stronger."

"I love you, Bella. So much."

"And I love you."

# EPILOGUE

*Three months later*

BELLA GLANCED AROUND the small ballroom with satisfaction at a job well executed and also with a very full heart. She'd seen to every bit of planning for the event. After all, it was their engagement party and she had wanted everything to be perfect.

Burke was beside her, looking dashing as ever in a tuxedo. She'd chosen a long dress in black velvet, reminiscent of Rosemary Clooney's in *White Christmas*. She'd always adored that style, and had even paired it with long satin gloves.

They'd invited friends and close business associates in addition to family. Right now, waitstaff was circulating with delectable nibbles and the champagne fountain was doing a brisk business. Aurora was chatting with Burke's mother; the two of them had rekindled their old friendship and had become quite inseparable. Charlotte was in attendance but moving slowly; her due date was three days past and she'd threatened to dance the jitterbug if it meant shaking the baby loose and getting things on the go. William and Gabi were gazing at each other, still in their cocoon of newlywed bliss, and Stephen...well, Bella was starting to think Stephen would be perennially single. Even Christophe wasn't immune to the romance in the air. He was currently chatting up Sophie Waltham, a gemologist whose family was a Bond Street jeweler who carried Aurora's jewelry line.

"Everyone looks so happy," she said to Burke, leaning against his arm. "It's lovely, isn't it?"

He tilted his head so that it rested briefly on hers. "It is. But no one is happier than me that you said yes."

The remainder of August had been a blur. Burke had taken the job at the hospital and moved to Paris and into her flat. Despite their earlier problems, they'd slid into living together seamlessly. When insecurities cropped up, they talked through them without walking away. It had only brought them closer together. Burke had proposed mid-October, presenting Bella with an heirloom diamond ring that had belonged to his grandmother. She was about to become Lady Downham after all.

Bella thought back to just six months ago and how everything had changed. And all because Burke had discovered her darkest secret and his acceptance had given her the push she needed to stop hiding. "You know, I didn't want to see you at Will's wedding. I certainly didn't want you to see my scars. But I'm so glad you did. You changed my life, Burke."

He kissed her temple. "And you changed mine. I love you, Bel. I always will."

And she believed him. Because she knew that sometimes the greatest risks, the biggest leaps of faith, yielded the very best rewards. In Bella's case, it was a happily-ever-after she thought she'd never have.

She turned her head and looked up at him. "Let's dance," she suggested, and when he took her in his arms on the dance floor, she knew anything was possible.

\* \* \* \* \*

*If you missed the previous stories in the Heirs to an Empire trilogy,
then check out*

**Scandal and the Runaway Bride
The Heiress's Pregnancy Surprise**

*And if you enjoyed this story,
check out these other great reads from
Donna Alward*

**The Billionaire's Island Bride
Beauty and the Brooding Billionaire
Christmas Baby for the Billionaire**

*All available now!*